That Shining Place
Simone Poirier-Bures

Copyright © 1995 by Simone Poirier-Bures

All rights reserved: no part of this book may be reproduced in any form or by any means, electronic or mechanical, except by a reviewer, who may quote brief passages in a review to be printed in a newspaper or magazine or broadcast on radio or television.

The author wishes to thank the Virginia Centre for the Creative Arts (VCCA) for providing a residency during which part of this work was written. An excerpt entitled "Crete 1966" was first published in *The Dalhousie Review*.

This book was published with the assistance of the Canada Council, the Ontario Arts Council and others.

ISBN 0 7780 1017 1 (hardcover)
ISBN 0 7780 1019 8 (softcover)

Cover art by Katherine Hansen
Book design by Michael Macklem

Printed in Canada

PUBLISHED IN CANADA BY OBERON PRESS

For Maria
And for Allen, who made the return possible

1

In the photo I remember, Maria looks straight at the camera. A smile flutters at the corners of her mouth, as if she is hesitant to show her ferocious pride, as if she dares not enjoy this moment, surrounded by her children, lest some jealous god yank it away. She rests her hands on the shoulders of Ireni, who barely comes up to her waist. Somber Ireni, whose eyes are large and unsmiling. Smaragdi and Katina stand at their mother's right, their heads reaching just to and just below her shoulders; Katina, distracted by something, looks off to the side. Yannis, at the left, is barely as tall as Smaragdi, though he is older than his sisters. He stands a little apart from the others, as if, as the only male, he feels a need to disassociate himself from the women.

There is something hopeful in their expressions, in the way they are poised there, their faces curious, expectant, as if they are used to standing on the sidelines watching, waiting for things to happen.

Behind them, the stuccoed wall is yellowish brown and peeling. It's the wall of my house, the one I occupied for four months, 25 years ago. Theirs, very much like mine, stands directly across the street. I remember also in this picture the hindquarters of a donkey, a brown shaggy one who carried things for the old man who delivered goods to the small store a few doors down, but perhaps I am confusing this photo with another.

Maria's husband Giorgos is missing from this family portrait, but that is usual. Every morning he would leave his house at dawn, return for the noon meal and a few hours rest, then leave again. He would spend his evenings in one of several *tavernas* along the waterfront. I seldom saw him at home, though I waved to him whenever I saw him along the old harbour, bringing in his catch. And he would wave back, in front of the other fishermen, giving a surprised but pleased smile to this young foreign woman. A friend of his wife's.

The *Yaya*, too, is absent. Maria's mother, all in black, would sit at her chair by the front window watching the goings on. Like all *Yayas*, she knew how to stay in the background, to help when there was work to be done, but otherwise, to remain invisible. I feel her hovering behind the photo, silently moving her toothless mouth.

They are all frozen in that moment—yet as I think of the picture, time softens, moves. Maria stands below my window, yelling "See-moan-ay! See-moan-ay!" It is 10.15 AM, far too late for decent people still to be sleeping, and anyway, she has something to tell me, or she is lonesome and wants some company, or it is the day for making some Greek delicacy, and I must come and watch so I can learn how.

It is 1966 and I am 21. I am in Chania, on the island of Crete, searching for something. Some truth that keeps eluding me. Some peace I long for. I am fleeing old griefs, trying to lose myself, find myself.

I am not completely alone; I am part of a small group of temporary expatriates—Canadians, Americans, Brits. We all live in the old quarter, in ancient three-storey houses built by the Venetians in the fourteenth and fifteenth centuries. We live there, instead of in the newer parts of the city where there are flush toilets and running water, because the streets in the old quarter are narrow and picturesque, because the rent is cheap, and because none of us cares about flush toilets and running water. We are all there for our own reasons—we do not ask each other such questions—and together we form a community of sorts. We go to the *tavernas* at night, dance with the sailors, drink too much, help each other find the way home.

Much of my day life, however, is with Maria. She has "claimed" me. When we walk through the neighborhood she holds my arm and tells the people we meet: "*Apo tin Ameriki.*" I correct her gently: from Canada. She shrugs and laughs. Wherever I am from, it does not matter. She was the first to have me in her house, so now I am known as "Maria's friend."

Come to my house for some *raki*, a woman down the street calls out to me. No, Maria says to her fiercely, she cannot. She is with me. Later, Maria tells me: that woman is not a good woman. But Athena, as she is called, will not give up so easily. When she sees me coming down the street without Maria, she rushes out to speak. She is thirtyish, a few years younger than Maria, but unmarried. She lives with her sister (also unmarried), and with her mother; occasionally she goes out with men from the nearby NATO base, and this makes her vaguely disreputable. I am curious about Athena, this loud, persistent woman who dyes her hair red, who hovers on the edge of respectability, but I do not wish to offend Maria, so I decline her invitations.

In the evenings, when I slip out to dance with the sailors on the waterfront, to drink, to behave in a way that is totally unacceptable for Greek women, I wonder what Maria thinks, at home, alone with her children. The rules are different for me; this is part of my appeal. Come with us, I say to her one Saturday evening when the winds are warm and we can smell spring coming. Giorgos never stays home—why should you? She clicks her tongue and throws her head back. I have proposed something preposterous, impossible. I might as well have proposed that we fly to the moon. She laughs, chides me for being so silly, but she puts on lipstick, and I know she is tempted.

At first I thought I was merely her trophy—something to show off in this city of few westerners. But Maria remained my friend long after it was expedient or prudent.

Mostly, I have forgotten the others, the ones I prowled the nights with. Only the odd name stays with me, a fragment of story, the antics of a particular evening. But I have not forgotten Maria—the heat I felt in her, the yearning. Her haunted eyes.

"See-moan-ay! See-moan-ay!" she yells through the front window. It is unshuttered and open because it is a lovely warm day, even in mid-January. Behind her stands Yannis, ready to supply the appropriate English if I do not understand what his mother tells me. He is eleven, small and sturdy, with a curious, intelligent face. He is learning English in school, and eager to try out his new words. When his friends invite him to play kickball down the street, he demurs, telling them he can't right now, that his mother needs his help. I understand enough Greek to catch this, and to know that we could manage without him. He looks at me shyly; I am not like Greek young women; I tease him, and he hides his smiles.

Maria's friend Varvara has invited us for coffee. I must come now. Varvara is one of the band of gypsies who winter over every year in Chania. I know this because I have seen her pull her small cart laden with colourful woven blankets and rugs through the narrow streets of the old quarter. She is short and compact like Maria, with dark fierce eyes like hers. But Varvara has a shrewdness about her. I do not trust her. A few weeks ago, I bought a blanket from her; later I discovered I had paid far too much.

I am surprised to learn that Varvara is Maria's "friend," as the gypsies are not well-liked here. Faces tighten, mouths curl as the gypsies pass. But I do not question this odd alliance. I, too, am an outsider, and I, too, am Maria's friend.

The gypsies are encamped behind the old city wall, a few minutes walk from our street. Yannis may not come, it is only for the women, Maria tells him. Yannis turns away in disappointment. The *Yaya*'s face appears in Maria's front window. She will watch the children. It is a beautiful afternoon and as we walk, I tell Maria about the blanket. She throws her head back and laughs. In Greece, anything is fair in business.

The path to the encampment takes us along the top of the old wall, now crowded with tiny, whitewashed shacks. In the five hundred years since the wall was built, the inner face has totally disappeared; the town has sloped up to meet it. Only when you stand at the edge and look down, do you realize that you are on a wall, and how high you are. Maria and I stand there for a moment, looking down. In the clearing below, about two dozen tents form a tiny village, complete with rickety-looking wooden wagons, a motley group of horses and donkeys, a few old cars. A trash fire burns on one side, downwind from the tents. A dog barks. It is eerie to see this scene, like something out of time, something from the Middle Ages. I want to express this observation to Maria, but it is too complicated for my simple Greek vocabulary, so I smile and squeeze her arm, and we follow the path down.

As we approach the camp, we become the focus of attention. I am suddenly aware of my long yellow hair hanging loosely to my waist, my blue eyes. The dark eyes of the men follow me, openly, aggressively. They resemble Greek men in their darkness, in their luxurious moustaches, but their faces are narrower, their cheekbones more pronounced. I hold Maria's arm more tightly. One of them asks us what we want there. Maria tells him in a loud voice that we are looking for Varvara's tent. He points the way. I realize, then, with a sudden twinge of fear, that Maria has never been here before. Is this all some elaborate trap? Has Varvara tricked Maria into bringing me here so that I can be stolen, then sold as a white slave? The youth hostels in Europe were full of such stories.

A man approaches us with a proprietary air. He jerks his head to the right, indicating that we follow him. He spreads his arms out and around us, as if to shield us from the curious eyes of the others. I feel Maria relax a little. Varvara's husband, she tells me.

Their canvas tent, like all the others, is a greyish, stained tan. Through the partly open front flap we see Varvara, who rises to greet us. We take off our shoes before we enter, leaving them with the others in a neat row outside. The inside is both roomy and cozy. Layers of blankets and rugs in patterns of bright blue, green and red pad the floor. Varvara and her husband exchange a few words in their own language; the husband darts a last look at me, then leaves, pulling the door flap down behind him.

Varvara invites us to sit down on the carpets and we do, forming a circle around a square slab that holds a small stove and a few cooking utensils. I am not sure what to expect from all this, but I suddenly realize that being invited here is a great honour. Maria seems to understand this too, and nods at me solemnly. Varvara lights the stove, a tiny one-burner, fuelled by gas. She takes a handful of coffee beans from a burlap bag, puts them in a flat, long-handled copper pan, and shakes them over the fire for a few minutes. The tent fills with a wonderful burnt-brown smell. While the beans cool, she opens a long brass cylinder and begins to assemble what I see now is a coffee grinder. It's a beautiful thing, obviously very old, the elaborate engraving well worn. I wonder for a moment, how many generations of gypsy women have owned this grinder, how many continents it has travelled.

As Varvara grinds the beans, the tent smells more and more aromatic. I wave my hand in front of my nose and say *"orea,"* beautiful, beautiful. Varvara nods at me gravely, but says nothing. She places a few spoonfuls of the powdered coffee with water into a small brass pot, then adds a few large spoonfuls of sugar. When the coffee froths up, she fills three small white cups, paper thin, and hands one each to Maria and me.

Now Varvara smiles. Welcome, my friends, she says. We sip our coffee slowly. Varvara inquires about Maria's family; Maria inquires back. She asks me about my health; I ask back. We are formal, ceremonial. Here, in her own element, Varvara is beautiful. She has loosened her hair and it hangs over her back in a thick mantle of glossy black. She looks softer than before, yet at the same time more powerful. I let the strong, sweet liquid linger on my tongue. Though I have had Greek coffee before, this is the best I have ever tasted. I am in a gypsy camp, I say to myself. A gypsy has called me "friend." I forgive Varvara for the blanket.

Maria and I never returned to the encampment—the gypsies moved on shortly after our visit—yet that time stands out as somehow emblematic. Maria was my guide, lifting up the corners of her world, letting me in.

In these 25 years, I have not always thought of Maria. Weeks, even months have passed without her presence in my consciousness. But whenever Greece is mentioned, or anything Greek, or when I make *dolmathes*, or *baklava*, or *kourabiethes*—all part of my regular kitchen repertoire now—Maria emerges from her small sacred place. And then I remember the dancing.

It is late afternoon, between four and five. The afternoon sleep is over and the men have returned to their shops or their boats for the second half of the work day. The children trickle home from school, idling along the street corners. Maria sits at her window, watching. She has finished most of her day's work, so all that remains is this sitting and watching, or perhaps a short *volta*, a walk around the harbour with one of the children if the evening is mild. Later on, around seven or eight, she will fix a simple meal for herself, her mother, and the children. Giorgos will eat at a *taverna* with his friends, and won't return until ten or eleven. A row of empty hours lies ahead. When she sees me coming down the narrow road Maria hurries out to meet me. *"Ella, ella!"* Come! Come! My arms are full of books and papers. In a moment, I tell her, laughing at her eagerness.

When I cross the street a few moments later, Maria removes her apron and smooths the front of her dress. During my first few weeks in Chania, each visit to Maria's house was rewarded with a saucer of thick, syrupy apricot preserves, and a small thin glass of *tsicoudia*, which Maria and her mother and Giorgos and the children solemnly watched me eat and drink. The liquid burned on the way down, made my face flush with heat and pleasure. We spoke mostly through nods and gestures, the language of host and guest. But now that Maria and I are "sisters," she brings out the preserves and brandy only on special occasions, or when there are other visitors.

Maria pushes the table and chairs to one side of the room, and goes to the shelf where she keeps her prize possession: a small boxy record player with a few dozen 45s. Suddenly the room fills with the piercing, electric sound of *bouzoukia*. Maria grabs my hand, Katina grabs the other, and with Smaragdi and Ireni we form a circle. The children have been expecting this, as a late-afternoon visit from me usually means dancing. Yannis declines to join us. If his friends were to pass, they would see him dancing with the women. The *Yaya* also watches from her chair, her face a mixture of amusement and disapproval. The music gets louder, the dancing more frantic. Yannis closes the front curtain and slips into the circle. The laughter gets more raucous, the room become a hot tunnel of wild, pounding sound. The music leaps out of the windows and into the street, drawing a handful of neighbourhood children who come in the front door, their eyes huge with excitement. Yannis no longer cares if anyone sees him. The circle swells and we bang and bump against each other laughing and panting. We do the *Sirtakia*, *Kalamatiano*, *Hassapo-serviko*— Maria knows them all. We dance and dance, until our legs turn to rubber, and we fall out laughing and exhausted.

There was something so incredibly joyful about this, all of us whirling madly on the grey cement floor of that crowded room, under the bare electric bulb that hung from the ceiling, as if we owned the world and nothing else mattered. I wanted to drown myself in this, and everything else Greek. The dances, the drink, the food. The passion of the Greeks. Their joy in being alive, their celebration of it. I wanted to absorb it, become it. Find out the secret. How to be happy, how to be free.

2

You come down through one of the narrow, twisting streets, barely wide enough for a small car, and you come upon it: the old harbour, opening before you like a flower. A wide paved area separates the buildings from the water, very much like an Italian piazza, which is appropriate, given that this part of Chania was built by the Venetians. At the edge of the piazza, the water is deep, and small fishing boats pull right up to the edge to unload their catches. Mid-morning they bring in the octopus. Glossy and silvery grey, raw octopus look like the internal organs of extraterrestials. There is something vaguely obscene about those thick, slimy appendages; cooked up, however, they are an amazing delicacy. The fishermen throw the octopus by the handfuls on to the pavement, then pick them up and throw them down again, beating them like this to release the dark blue inky substance, and to tenderize them. The octopus are then hung on makeshift racks and lines to dry, and the fishermen wash down the pavement with buckets of sea water.

Sometimes it's sea urchins they bring in, one or two buckets of them, their greenish grey shells bristling with needle-sharp spines. Inside, flesh the colour of smoked salmon. I have never tried them—they are food for the wealthy—though I am told they are wonderful. Mostly though, the boats are full of fish and octopus, and all morning the air is briny and aromatic. By noon, all trace of the fishermen is gone.

Everything around the old harbour is a bit shabby. The façades of some of the buildings have begun to crumble. Old paint peels from walls and woodwork like outgrown skin. Some of the buildings are whitewashed, but most are not, unlike the picture postcards one sees of sparkling white Greek villages. Here the buildings are mostly a drab gold—the colour of limestone—or light ochre, or the greyish tan of unpainted cement.

Still, there is something enormously pleasing about it all. The crowded buildings face the water like flowers facing the sun. Roofs of red tile and wide doors painted a glossy blue flash patches of colour. Old oil cans grow huge red geraniums. The rounded domes of an ancient mosque, a legacy of the Turkish occupation, shimmer in the sun like white hills. A bright green fishing boat moors on the water. Everything seems harmonious, comforting. On fine days, the restaurants spill out into the piazza. Tables and chairs appear on the pavement, inviting. On weekends, the aroma of roasting meat fills the air.

On my way home from the *Instituto*, I stop at one of the sweet shops for a *galato-buriko*, or a bowl of rice custard, or a piece of *baklava*, and look out at the harbour water. Sometimes blue, sometimes black, the water riffles lightly or bristles with foam, depending on its mood. Though the ancient sea wall contains it—a small opening permits the comings and goings of small boats—the harbour water is never totally placid, more like some wild thing, barely domesticated. And it seems emblematic somehow, of all of Crete: hungers surge up, then subside, waiting for their own good time. A thin layer of order overlays roiling chaos—Apollo and Dionysious held in delicate balance.

"Chania has changed since you lived there," our friends in Athens say. "It's full of tourists now. You won't recognize it."

It is April, 1991, and my husband and I have just arrived in Athens. We are showing each other places in Greece and Turkey we knew and loved a lifetime ago when we were both different selves. We have only a few weeks for these explorations, so our days are full, intense.

The friends in Athens have studied in the States, are worldly, sophisticated. They are also ten years younger than we, not yet haunted by the need to revisit landscapes of the past. I tell them about Maria, my hope of finding her, show them the box of chocolates I have brought for her, heart-shaped and garishly decorated, the sort of thing I am sure she would like. They smile, give each other little looks. Twenty-five years is a long time.

I have not written to Maria to tell her we are coming, for I don't know when, exactly, we will arrive, nor do I have any idea of the circumstances of her life. I do not wish to burden her with an old friendship, with the implicit demands that an announcement of our arrival might contain. It is possible that she no longer lives in Chania. It is possible that she no longer lives. And though I can barely conceive of the idea, it is possible that she no longer remembers me.

We will knock on the door of her old house, I tell our friends, since we will be there anyway, looking at mine, across the street from hers. If we do not find her, we can always give the chocolates to someone else.

"I hope you won't be disappointed," they say. But I cannot conceive of disappointment. Just being in Greece again seems a kind of miracle, this return to the scene of my life's great adventure, my life's great experiment. The memories crowd around me, ghosts bobbing up to the surface, eager to show themselves once more. I greet them with love and chagrin and longing, that time, so full of dark and light.

And now we are here, aboard the Knossos, the huge ferry that will take us across the sea of Crete, once more to Chania.

We have booked a cabin for the overnight trip, a tidy compact room with two bunks. The Knossos is an old ship, as the thickly varnished wood attests, perhaps the very same ship I made one of several crossings on, 25 years ago. We pour ourselves some brandy and stroll out to explore. It's a huge, mutilayered thing, capable of carrying more than a hundred cars and semi-trucks. It sleeps several hundred passengers in various types of accommodations represented by a complex system of classes.

Twenty-five years ago, only one class was possible for me: deck class. The deck is much as I remembered, rows of benches enclosed in a large room, and under a sheltered canopy outside. People are settling in, claiming certain benches near the windows and doors, establishing the boundaries of their territory with backpacks, shopping-bags, battered suitcases. There are only a few dozen deck passengers tonight, and as before, they consist of a mixture of poor Greeks and young tourists. Though black-clothed *Yayas* and old men formed the staple of those crossings years ago, few of tonight's passengers are elderly. Clearly, people are more prosperous now. The standards have changed. A pair of young women in jeans and thick sweaters, both of them lean and a bit shabby, show the marks of seasoned travellers. I stare at the one with long, yellowish hair, and for a brief, strange moment, it is like seeing my younger self. I have a sudden urge to ask her name, to tell her: I was you, 25 years ago. A handful of young men, some Greek, some tourists of various nationalities, are also claiming benches, and before the night is over, I know there will be conversations, laughter, an exchange of adventures and liquor, maybe even some new alliances formed. This is the way it was. That easy sharing, that ability to enter and leave someone else's life, richer for it, yet unencumbered.

I don't remember now, whom I made that first crossing with. Some boy I'd met at the Athens youth hostel, perhaps, who later went his own way. I had come to Europe by myself and most of the other young women, already in pairs, were not looking for a third female, so I travelled mostly with young men. Whenever I could, I travelled with two; that way things were more likely to remain uncomplicated. I remember of that first crossing only that it was a cold, early November night, and that I slept in my thin sleeping-bag on the outside deck, because the inside deck was thick with smoke and smelled of food and vomit. Someone came by with a bottle of *ouzo*, and there was low talk. I remember the tilting ship, the brilliant stars, the gentle lapping of Homer's wine-dark sea.

Part of me wants to hunker down with those young deck passengers, spend the night there listening to their stories.

But I think of my cozy cabin, the comfortable bed. Besides, I already know their stories. Twenty-five years ago, the youth hostels were full of such adventurers. We were mostly young, in our late teens and early twenties, hordes of us, tromping through Europe, the Middle East, North Africa. What were we looking for? Strangeness, perhaps. Something other than the ordinary. We floated from country to country, unconnected, like clouds of wispy dandelion seeds.

Vietnam was just beginning then, and most of us were only vaguely aware of it. The European students seemed to know more about it than did anyone I knew back home in Halifax, or in Boston, where I had attended college. But it was no concern of mine, this war; it belonged to the Americans. I had my own darkness. Among other things, I was full of the angst that came of living in northern climates by the sea, where the mornings were thick with fog, and it seemed always to be winter. I wanted warmth. I wanted something "other."

In Iraklion a woman in her late thirties, a former housewife, told of leaving a husband and suburban home in Australia. Travelling with her twelve-year-old son, it had taken her six months to get this far, stopping as she did to work a bit here and there, to raise the fare for the next leg of the trip. I remember being shocked by her, by the discovery that when you reached adulthood things were not automatically fixed. The malaise, the restless yearning I felt might not be simply a passage of youth. This was a frightening thought. The woman was housekeeping now for the youth-hostel owner, a widower in his forties, and judging from his proprietary smile, I guessed she would stay for a while.

I was shocked by her, but also impressed. What did social structures mean, after all? All this grasping and organizing, this constricting of possibilities: this way or that way, but not both. In the youth-hostel kitchen I watched her stir a huge pot of vegetable soup. Her thick brown hair hung past her shoulders in a reckless, girlish way. No grown woman I knew back home had hair like that. Like her, I decided, I would make my own life. Like her, I would make it any way I pleased.

I had been both driven and pulled to Greece. There had to be meaning somewhere, anywhere but in the tight grey cities and Catholic schools where I had spent my life so far. I had been reading Katzanzakis, and he, in part, drew me to Greece and Crete. In Iraklion, I stood for a long time at his grave overlooking the harbour, pondering the words etched on his small stone: I want nothing, I fear nothing, I am free.

I had already begun to free myself, mostly from the tyranny of things. Experience, I told myself, was more important than possessions. I had left my four suitcases with the owner of a brasserie in Brussels, my first European stop, and taken with me only a small backpack and my guitar. When I got to Chania and decided to stay, I resolved to keep my life spartan.

I meant to strip down life to its essentials. See what remained. Somehow I felt that in ridding myself of the encumbrance of things and of daily comforts, I would rid myself of my past and all its old enclosures. It would be like starting over, newly born.

Before settling in Chania and meeting Maria, I had already fallen in love with Crete and its inhabitants. With a young Brit I met at the Iraklion youth hostel, I set off to visit the site of every Minoan ruin on the island. Many were located in obscure areas not visited by westerners for many years. Once, we found ourselves thronged by villagers. Swarthy hands touched me, stroked my yellow hair; dark faces pushed toward me, only inches away from my own. I froze in fear. "Take it easy," my companion said. "They've never seen anything like you before."

When I calmed down enough to notice, I saw that the faces were full of wonder and admiration, and that only the women were touching. *"Orea,"* they were saying, over and over. Beautiful. We were half pushed, half pulled to a low whitewashed cottage, consisting of two rooms, one with a huge open hearth. A few low stools stood on the hard dirt floor, and a man gestured for us to sit down. He barked some instruction to a boy who hurried out of the hut and returned a few moments later clutching four eggs to his chest. The man made a gesture of eating. Evidently, and to our relief, for we were very hungry, they intended to feed us.

A woman, presumably the man's wife, squatted over a low fire in the open hearth. In a huge black skillet she sliced large chunks of raw potato into bubbling olive oil. When they were cooked, she removed them on to a cracked plate and broke the eggs into the oil. The man and the boy continued to stare openly at us, as did what seemed like half the village population. They had followed us there, and now stood at the open door and window looking in. Our host's thick black moustache and black eyes twitched with satisfaction.

When the eggs were cooked, the woman served us each a plate of fried potatoes and eggs drenched with olive oil, and a large chunk of bread. The man and woman and boy made no signs of joining us. We tried to gesture "sharing" or "eating together" but the man and woman threw their heads back and clicked their tongues. So we ate, while dozens of dark eyes watched silently. When night came, we unfolded our sleeping-bags on the floor and slept; I dreamed of eyes, hovering over me, and felt oddly protected.

In the morning there was coffee, thick and sweet, and more bread. The other villagers had disappeared from the windows and door, and the street was empty. It was as if the whole village had been abandoned during the night, and only our host and his son remained. As we were leaving, my companion held out a few pieces of paper money to the man, but he threw back his head, insulted. I then remembered the two Hershey bars in my knapsack and offered those to the boy. He looked to his father before he put out his hand. His father nodded, and the boy took the chocolate bars, holding them like sacred objects.

Perhaps it was this incident that decided me on Crete. The simplicity of it. The generosity. Among such people, surely I would find what I was seeking.

Now, standing on the deck of this ageing ship, watching the moonlight ripple off the sea, making the wave tips an almost florescent white, I try to recall the darkness that hovered over my 21st year. The darkness I hoped the light in Crete would dispel. The old rooms are familiar; I know them intimately. But the actual aroma of suffering is gone. I grieved a young man who had forsaken me. My father's death. The loss of my religious faith. The materialism of the western world. Its extraordinary waste. Its lack of real joy.

I settled in Chania by luck. On our perigrinations around the island in search of Minoan sites, my young British friend and I had been joined by another young man from England. Jack was a painter, and after the first young man went back to Athens, Jack and I continued on to Chania. Winter was coming. We had heard that on the western part of the island, the climate was milder. In addition to olive trees, there were vineyards, orange groves, pomegranate and banana trees. I had never seen a banana tree in my life, and suddenly wanted to see one more than anything.

The youth hostel in Chania was in a boys' school, and consisted of one room with three sets of bunk beds, separated from one of the classrooms by pieces of cardboard and a plastic shower curtain. An American boy, who had preceded us by one day, was the only other guest. Each morning, at 8.30, we would wake to the sounds of classes going on in the room on the other side of the cardboard/shower curtain wall. The toilet, which served the school as well, was on the other side of a large courtyard; a small outside sink with cold running water provided the only place to wash. Every morning while I washed my face and brushed my teeth, an audience of about 50 black-eyed boys watched me. A small room off the sleeping-room contained a hot plate, making it possible for us to prepare light meals. To bathe, we had to go to the public baths.

On our second morning there, we were visited by another young man from England. I remember wondering in those days whether there were any males under the age of 28 still left in Britain, for I encountered so many of them in my travels. He taught at a small Greek/American language school in Chania, and wanted to go back to England. He had been visiting the youth hostel every few days looking for a newcomer who could replace him, so he could leave with a clear conscience. He pounced on me when he learned that I had just finished a degree in English. "You'd be perfect," he told me. "They'll love you."

It was often chilly and rainy in the mornings. I had been travelling for six weeks, staying no more than two or three nights in any one place. I was tired, ready for a rest, and I sensed that Crete possessed what I needed. Chania seemed as good a place as any, and with an income, I could stay as long as I wanted.

Jack planned to stay in Chania for about six months. He carried his paints and rolled up canvases in his backpack, and only needed to find a place to rent. So we prowled the old quarter together and found a house that had been vacant for some time. Like most of the Venetian houses, it consisted of three floors, two rooms to a floor. It was partially furnished: a cot on the third floor, a wooden bench-sofa on the second floor, and a table and three chairs in the front room on the first floor. Jack would take the top floor, I would take the middle floor, and we would share the ground floor with its ancient kitchen. We were "just friends," we agreed; our arrangement would remain one of simple convenience. I would stay for at least a few months; we would share the $20 a month rent.

When Maria stopped us in the street the next day to welcome us, we told her we were husband and wife. The differences in our accents would arouse suspicion only in an English-speaker. Later, when it was no longer convenient to have Jack as my "husband," (I had begun to haunt the *tavernas* with other friends, to stroll along the harbour with Greek sailors), I told Maria we were cousins, that we were travelling together because my father, before dying, had asked him to take care of me. I had gotten the words mixed up, I shrugged. Husband, good heavens, Maria, what a silly mistake. Maria looked at me quizzically—how could anyone mistake a thing like that? But she questioned me no further. By then she loved me; in her eyes, I could do no wrong.

3

My house: generations have lived here, stretching back, perhaps, to the fourteenth century. What were they like, those Venetians who occupied Crete, who built Chania's splendid harbour, the ancient sea wall, and those tall, stately rowhouses? And how did they make their comforts in these rooms, especially those in the back, where there are no windows to bring in the light? On rainy days I can hardly stand to be in the kitchen, everything dark and clammy, only a bare bulb hanging from the ceiling, and that only recent. On sunny days, with the windows in the front room unshuttered and thrown open, the light reaching back along the cement floor, I think of the women who have cooked at the huge, elevated hearth where I keep my small one-burner stove. Sometimes I am tempted to make a roaring fire in the hearth, heat up the room and watch the crackling light, as if it would illuminate the faces of those women, draw them from their hidden places. What would they tell me of their lives? What would they say was important—then, now, always? Firewood, in any case, is almost impossible to find, and I doubt that the chimney still works.

To the side of the hearth stands a cement sink, with a drain that leads to a bucket below. Over the sink hangs a metal water canister with a spigot. In the corner, a cement cistern holds the general water supply, into which I dip a pot for cooking or washing. A tube in the wall, also with a spigot, connects to the cistern with a piece of rubber hose. Water flows from the tube into the cistern for two hours, three days a week. We have to remember to turn the spigot on and off on those days, if we want to replenish our water supply.

The metal canister is a recent addition, in the previous ten years perhaps, though something like it, probably in ceramic, must have been used for centuries back. The hearth, the cistern and the sink I imagine to be original, though surely they could not be. Still, there must have been some way to store water, some area for washing, and that good, solid hearth would have to have been built with the house.

Off the kitchen, where a back entrance to the house might once have been, a white porcelain toilet sits under an awning of corrugated metal. A bucket of water poured into it makes it flush.

Has there always been water like that, coming into the house from some mysterious network of waterways? I ask Maria, wondering at the inventive Venetians, for their building prowess is legendary. Maria shrugs. And what did people do before there were toilets, all those hundreds of years before? Maria laughs, cuffs me gently, as if I am a pesky fly with all my strange questions. Maria's kitchen and toilet are much the same as mine, though everything is cheerier, with flowered cotton curtains separating one area from the rest. Her ancient hearth is boarded over and the area hung with pots and pans; she has two one-burner stoves with which to prepare meals for her family of six. Rough, wooden shelves, also covered with curtains, form counter tops and storage areas. Everything in Maria's house is cleaner, lighter, well-used.

Slowly, some of the old Venetian houses were being renovated, modernized. Some of the older foreigners lived in such houses, with shower stalls in real bathrooms, ceramic kitchen sinks with chrome faucets, space heaters to take off the winter chill. Sometimes I longed for heat, light, the comfort of a hot bath. But I resisted. Maria and most of the others on my street managed without them. To me, their lives were closer to the real thing.

I hated the part of myself that cringed from things. When I woke up on a cold, rainy morning in my unheated house, I hated whatever it was that kept me lying there, unable to get up. Maria, I knew, would leap out of bed on such mornings, and hurry down to light the charcoal brazier to heat the kitchen. And on warm, sunny mornings, she would throw open her windows, fling the bedclothes over the balcony to air, and sweep the whole house—all while I lay on my hard bed, telling myself to get up.

Downstairs, I fumble with the small stove to heat some water for tea. While it heats, I open the front shutters to let in the sun. Passing under the archway that separates the kitchen from the front room, I keep my eye on the large colony of spiders who nest in a corner up there. They are enormous, furry and black, and each time I pass under, I pull my collar tightly closed and hurry. I imagine them watching me warily—those original tenants—resenting my presence. I don't wish to share the house with them, but don't know how to get them to leave. For a month now, we have lived this uncomfortable truce.

Maria, who is now busily sweeping the street in front of her house, notices my open shutter. "*Simonay! Kali mera!*" she calls over. I open the door and we exchange greetings. When I hear my water boiling, I rush back to the kitchen to shut off the stove, casting a nervous eye, as usual, at the top of the doorjamb as I pass under. Maria, watching this, is curious. She follows me into the room to look. I point at the spiders and shudder. Maria laughs and swings her broom, and before I realize what is happening, spiders are raining down around us and scuttling across the floor while Maria swats them. I shriek and jump around the room, trying to hold my hands over my head and pull my skirt around my legs, all at the same time. They are only spiders, Maria says, *arachne*, and laughs and laughs until her cheeks are wet.

Maria's voice: When she stood on the street calling my name, looking up at my shuttered windows, her voice rushed out from somewhere deep inside her body. Her short, almost square body, anchored solidly on the earth. Her voice rose up through her body from the earth. Her voice was a deep, husky river from under the rich, dark Cretan earth.

"*Ella, Simonay!*" Maria's waving hands are covered with flour. I must come and see. A huge bowl rests on her kitchen table flanked by two enormous, heavy cookie sheets. On one sits a half dozen egg-shaped lumps of dough. Ireni, who at four is not yet in school, stands on a chair, carefully sticking a whole clove into each shape. "*Kourabiethes,*" Maria explains excitedly. I recognize these as the delicious butter cookies I am sometimes presented with, one at a time, on a small glass plate, during a visit here, or at some other Greek home. After the cookies are baked at the public oven down the street, Maria will roll each one in powdered sugar.

I nod, but Maria is not convinced I have understood. She says something to Ireni, who scurries off to the back room and returns with a large tin box. Inside are two of the familiar cookies, half buried in powdered sugar.

"*Kourabiethes,*" Maria says again.

"*Kourabiethes!*" I repeat, nodding and laughing. She points, then, to a bowl of butter. "*Vootero,*" she says, and waits until I say the word after her.

"Mama Maria," I say, laughing.

"No, sister," Maria says in English. "You are my sister."

I hold a piece of my long yellow hair next to Maria's dark curly hair. "Sisters," I agree, and we both throw back our heads and laugh. Ireni stares at us with large solemn eyes.

In one of the two rooms on the second floor of my house stood an elaborate wooden bar, padded with tufted red plastic, the kind of thing you might find in the basement recreation-room of a middle-class American home. It looked new, and in my view, incredibly ugly and garish. Where did it come from? It belonged to the previous tenant, the landlord explains. A man named Beel who had not actually lived in the house, but had rented it for two months. He would be returning to get the bar, the landlord tells us. Sometime soon.

Where is Beel? Athena wants to know. Have we seen him lately? We have no idea who he is, we tell her. He is an American, she informs us, so we must know him. Though Jack is British and I am Canadian and we have both only just arrived, it doesn't seem to matter. All the foreigners are expected to know one another. When we see Beel, we are to tell him that Athena was asking about him, she says. She is a big woman, barrel-chested. When she talks to you, it is hard not to pay attention.

"Who is Beel?" I ask some of the other foreigners.

"Oh, Bill. He's this coloured guy stationed at the NATO base out here somewhere. Haven't seen him in a while."

"What was he doing with a bar in that house?"

"He wanted to turn it into a little love nest. Thought he could seduce Greek women if he had a place to take them. I guess it didn't work out quite the way he planned."

This strikes me as extremely funny. That cold uncomfortable house as a love nest. I might have thought of constructing a plush, elaborate bed as a lure, installing a good heater, perhaps. But a bar? I stack my belongings on it, spread out my toiletries on the inside shelf, thinking: how typically male, how typically American.

A few weeks later, Bill appears. He is thirtyish, fairly light-skinned, not particularly good-looking, but not ugly either. Do we still have his bar? Yes, has he come to retrieve it? Well, he was wondering if we might want to buy it. It's brand new, after all. No, we have no interest in buying it, he can take it any time. He has no place to keep it, he confesses. He lives on the base and shares a room with someone else.

"Athena asked about you," I tell him. "She seems very interested in you."

"That red-headed woman? Yeah, she's a trip." He looks over his shoulder. "Don't tell her you saw me."

I find it hard to picture this small, wiry man with the formidable Athena. That Athena would consider him a prize. But he is "American," and this in itself makes him a good catch. I note, with some satisfaction, that not once did a Greek mention the colour of his skin. He is freer here than he would be at home; he is one of us, the foreigners, and in their view, we are all the same.

My clothes: two dark, printed cotton flared skirts that fell a few inches below my knees; two short-sleeved cotton blouses and a long-sleeved one; a burgundy mohair bulky V-neck; one bra; four or five pairs of underpants; a bright red pair of pantaloons, meant to wear under trouser skirts, but which I wore under everything; a navy blue belted trenchcoat; a worn but sturdy brown shoulder bag, a hand-me-down from one of my mother's friends. Socks? Shoes? Nightgown? I don't remember. At Christmas, my sister back home in Nova Scotia went to great expense to send me a burgundy-and-grey plaid wool A-line skirt with a matching beret she had made for me. It was a welcomed gift; I had never imagined Greece could be so cold in winter. I bought a grey wool turtleneck sweater to match and felt like a princess in that outfit.

I had made a conscious decision *not* to wear pants on my travels, in deference to the cultural values of the countries I visited. I had never owned a pair of blue jeans, though they were the preferred costume of most of my fellow travelers, male and female alike. The skirts I wore were four or five inches too long to be fashionable in Canada and the United States, but just right for Greece. I was careful to keep my shoulders covered when I went out.

I wore my hair in a long thick braid, or in two thinner braids coiled and pinned on top of my head, or loose, cascading down my back.

I washed my underwear and the occasional blouse in a pan of warmed water. I must have washed my socks, too, though I don't remember that. I bathed with a pan of warmed water as well, and washed my hair every week or ten days. My grooming untensils were simple: a brush, comb, toothbrush and toothpaste, a dark brown eyebrow pencil which served as an eyeliner, a few rubber bands to tie up my hair. It was enough. I never felt dirty or deprived. And I never missed the contents of my four suitcases, stored in the basement of the brasserie in Brussels.

Every *thing* I bought I suffered over. Books, writing materials, food and drink didn't count; they were necessities. But anything else—clothes, personal ornaments, things for the house that were not absolutely essential—had to survive a long process of justification before I would open my purse. I would look at a bracelet or a pair of leather shoes in a shop window, and as I felt acquisitiveness seep through me, I would remind myself of the daughters of the wealthy I had spent my college years with. From their abundance they didn't miss the coats, leather gloves, mohair sweaters, wool skirts, silk blouses, scarves and jewellery they misplaced. Their things sat unclaimed for months in the dormitory's Lost and Found. At the end of each semester the Lost and Found would hold a sale, and I, the scholarship student, could buy a camel hair coat for a dollar, a silk blouse and skirt for seventy-five cents, a pair of kid gloves for a quarter. My four abandoned suitcases were full of these cheaply acquired things the daughters of the wealthy had lost and did not miss.

I had benefitted from their wastefulness, but I did not want to be like them. I had saved my money in quarters and dollars from summer waitressing jobs not to buy new clothes, but to buy my freedom, and to see the world. The four suitcases held almost everything I owned, clothing for every season, as I intended to stay away a long time. But even from the first day they seemed like chains, binding me to one place. It was not hard to leave them behind.

Freedom, after all, was wanting nothing, fearing nothing. Maria, too, wore the same cotton dress day after day, as did most of the other women in the old quarter. And the men wore the same trousers and shirts. They were the free ones; they were truly alive.

In my four months in Greece, I bought: the red and green blanket from Varvara; a red, gold and black Cretan wool bag; one of the beautiful silver and turquoise bracelets Greece is noted for. Over each, I agonized long and hard. Finally, I bought them because they were beautiful, and because they were Greece. Before leaving, I bought a few more pieces of Greek jewellery and textiles to take home to my sister and mother.

Varvara's blanket disappeared some fifteen years ago in the shuffle of a move. I still wear the silver and turquoise bracelet. The woollen bag, its cords now frayed, hangs from a hook behind my study door. The bracelet and bag serve as talismans—visible connections to that earlier time, that earlier self.

Jack had achieved more easily than I the freedom that comes from wanting nothing. His wardrobe was even more spartan than mine: two pairs of blue jeans, two shirts, a bulky navy sweater and two pairs of socks. He washed his socks out every few weeks, and hung them to dry over a chair, or on the roof. He wore a beard and moustache, so shaving equipment was unnecessary. His diet, too, was simpler than mine: he made a soup from garbanzo beans and onions, and ate it with bread every day of the week. The occasional egg, and a little pasta with tomato sauce rounded out his diet. Garbanzos and onions were cheap, so his food cost only a few cents a day. He allowed himself a night out every week or two, but even then, he bought only inexpensive things to eat and drink—perhaps a salad or a small plate of *dolma* with a few glasses of *ouzo*, as opposed to the more expensive *brisoles* and bottles of *retsina* the rest of us indulged in. He had calculated how many days he could stay in Crete if he lived like this, and he seldom wavered. He spent his money on more important things like paints, brushes and canvases.

I occasionally shared my feta cheese, oranges, tomatoes and figs with him, but for the most part, we rarely ate at the same time. In fact, after the first few weeks, we didn't see each other very much. He rose early and made his breakfast while I still slept. By the time I got up, he was already quietly painting on the third floor, or he had taken his paints and canvas and gone out into the country. When he came in to fix his supper, I was often walking, or visiting Maria, or on my way to the *tavernas*. I visited the third floor where he lived maybe two or three times in the four months we shared the house.

He never complained about his living conditions. He seemed untempted by the comforts and foods and things that tempted me. And he was always cheerful.

I wanted to be in love with him. It would have made things so much easier. But I felt no attraction that way, and often found his English cheerfulness cloying. It struck me as shallow, chirping, like the sound from a tinny radio. The Greeks, in comparison, were more like the full-throated sound from an expensive stereo. He was like something in the treetops whose feet never touched the ground; the Greeks were the thing that comes up from the earth to the tops of the mountains and roars. Perhaps it was only that he made living simply seem easy, when for me it was painfully difficult. That he succeeded where I faltered.

I don't think I ever saw any of his paintings.

In these 25 years I have often dreamed of my old house. Sometimes the rooms are like a labyrinth, one opening into another and another, and I cannot find my way. Sometimes I am trapped in the house: the doors won't open, and huge black spiders huddle in the corners, watching me. The walls are crumbling, and nothing works quite right. My former husband is sometimes in these dreams, and sometimes my son. Always, I have failed them in some important way.

In other dreams, I am looking for Maria. I have come back to Crete searching for something I have lost. She will know where it is. I inquire all through the old neighbourhood, but no-one has heard of her. Or Giorgos has died, and no-one knows what has happened to Maria.

Now that a reunion with Maria is actually possible, I find it hard to picture. Somehow, though, I imagine an opening, like a door to old rooms that have been closed up but left intact. Everything there, suspended, waiting to start up again.

And yet another reunion is implicit in all this. Waiting with Maria in that closed room is my younger self. She, I find, is the one who intrigues and frightens me. Some principle of being joins me to her, yet I cannot find what it is. Never again have I been so brave, so idealistic. Much of my life has been a sliding into, rather than a deliberate choosing; much of my life has been what others have wanted for me.

Though I am still attracted to the simple, I do not live simply. Though I have tried to resist the impulse to acquire, I live in a large, airy house with central air and heat, and three bathrooms, all of which have flush toilets. My life is ballasted by scattered acres of land, complicated accounts. I teach at the local university, live quietly, go to bed early; at least twenty years have passed since I danced in public with a stranger. It seems hardly possible that my younger self and I could have inhabited the same body, the same life.

I imagine a scene with two women: One is 46, has light brown hair streaked with grey, curled into a bob. She is still attractive, wears only a little makeup, though there is something *soignée* about her—the dangling earrings, a scarf arranged for effect. She has settled certain things in her life, made certain compromises. She is the visitor.

The other woman stands at an open door. She is 21, has long yellow hair that hangs limply, that needs to be washed more often. Behind her brown-rimmed glasses, her blue eyes are lined with black, making them look narrow, as if she is constantly weighing, constantly measuring things. Her skirt and blouse are rumpled, carelessly thrown on. She stands there awkwardly. She has been waiting for the older woman for a long time.

The two women eye each other. The older woman feels a rush of embarrassment. She wants to run to the younger woman, tell her: *You don't have to suffer so much. Nothing matters that much.* The younger woman looks at the older one, intensely curious but also embarrassed. *You seem like all the others,* she thinks. *Is this what it will come to?*

I do not know what they will say to each other when they speak.

4

December, in Crete, is the dreariest month. A cold drizzle falls; temperatures linger in the forties and fifties. The restaurants on the waterfront are deserted, gloomy; the sea looks sullen and irritable, like a cold hungry animal. There is not even Christmas to look forward to. In Greece, Easter is the big celebration; Christmas passes by with only a nodding notice. The community of foreigners has caught the doldrums. This won't do. We are in Greece, after all. We have a plan.

Several of the restaurants along the old harbour have huge rotating spits upon which they roast whole young lambs or piglets on request for weddings or celebrations, or from which to serve diners on pleasant evenings. We order a suckling pig, each chipping in our share of *drachma*, for a Christmas Eve feast. The pig is slowly roasted all day, and around six we carry it home on a door we have removed from its hinges and covered with oilcloth. On the way, someone starts chanting a Latin funeral dirge, and those among us who know the words join in. Through the narrow streets we go, carrying our pig and chanting. The *Yayas* look out from their windows. A light drizzle falls, but we do not feel it. Tonight, we are part of something larger than ourselves.

There are eight of us, for I remember four on each side of our makeshift table—the door, now set on two sawhorses. Our hosts are Basil and Marian, a couple in their early thirties—he on sabbatical from an American university, she, finishing a dissertation on some area in psychology. My housemate Jack is there, and Bryan, a fellow Canadian. Is Nora, the Irish woman, among us? I can still see her face and hear the sound of her voice, for she later taught me two haunting Irish songs. But I don't remember her presence that evening.

Marian has made some applesauce. There must be other kinds of food as well, but I remember only the pig and the apple sauce, and bottle upon bottle of *retsina*. Someone passes around a joint and everything becomes extremely funny—the door on two sawhorses, the pig on it, how we begin to grab at the pig with our bare hands, tearing it apart, gnawing at hunks of meat, throwing the bones over our shoulders. The laughter comes in gales, the bones thunk behind us on the floor; the bottles of *retsina* empty and are followed by *ouzo*. Much later, staggering home in the rain, Marian calls behind us: come back tomorrow and help clean up!

How hard we worked on joy and abandon. The Greeks achieved it without trying. The next day, achy and hungover, the old heaviness flowed back around me like dark water.

I walked a lot. Mornings when I had no lessons to prepare, afternoons when I didn't teach, or early evenings before it was time to go to the *tavernas*, I often headed out past the houses into the countryside. Sometimes I walked with one of the other foreigners; mostly I walked alone. Always the questions followed. What is the self? How does one live? What is necessary and what is not? How does one fill the deep hole that faith once occupied? And those darker matters—loneliness, sex, love.

Sometimes I begged my father, wherever he was, to give me a sign, to let me know if what I had stopped believing was actually true. *If you ever loved me, you will do this.*

The terrain, just beyond town, was rugged and scrubby. Wild oregano, thyme, rosemary, sage, basil and mint grew in great wild clumps, and when I brushed against them their fragrances leaped into the air. I had met only the dried variety of these herbs before—pale, dessicated objects in small, expensive bottles. The real thing, ripe and green and opulent, astounded me. Sometimes I would sit on a low rock, or lie down near a clump of something aromatic and stare at the sky. Soon there were only the bees, their buzz a high-pitched roar, and the wonderful, intoxicating scent—no questions, no temptations, no internal debates. Above, the blue sky looked down, silent and forgiving.

The market in Chania: a huge quonset-type structure, with a high, vaulted metal ceiling. Inside, small stalls line the walls, where vendors display their wares: Vats of honey, preserves, olive oil, *ouzo, raki,* neatly arranged piles of onions, eggplant, fava beans, lemons, oranges, tomatoes, eggs, nuts, figs, chunks of feta, mounds of ricotta, meats, whole fish—all beautifully displayed. People bring their own jars and bottles to be filled. Cheeses and meats are wrapped in paper, and carried, along with loose fruits and vegetables, in a cloth sack or a basket. Nothing is wasted. Everything is used and reused. Here, the smallest thing—an empty jar—has value.

After a week or two of drizzle or overcast skies, a sunny day comes like an explosion. Every shutter is thrown open, stoops are swept, bedding flung over the balcony railings to air. Up and down the street the flat rooftops sprout lines, drooping with wet linen and clothing. The doves and pigeons in their wire cages coo joyfully. The *Yaya* down the street washes her hip-long grey hair and hangs it to dry over the back of a wooden chair. There in a private place between two lines of clothes, she closes her eyes and holds her face up to the sun. Everyone smiles. *The air! The light!*

And the cats! Dozens of them, curling in sunny corners, their faces blinking in happiness. Homeless, they roam the neighbourhood, keeping it free of mice, disdaining the domestic comforts that their western cousins enjoy. If you stoop to pat one, it eyes you suspiciously. If you try to pick one up, it flees in terror. On overcast days you rarely see them; on sunny days, they are everywhere.

How happy, these small joys, these small beauties. To know with the body every small gift.

Bryan was the one who started me going to the *tavernas*. He had been in Crete longer than any of the rest of us, and lived at the end of my street, on the second floor of a Venetian house that had been made into a simple but comfortable apartment. He was 28 or 29, had toffee-coloured hair, ruddy skin, high cheekbones and glasses. His intense look reminded me of former seminarians I had known. Witty and articulate, he was the only foreigner who had studied as much Latin and Theology as I had, and who shared with me the same ferocious, lapsed faith.

He comes to the house one Saturday evening. He is on his way to a favourite *taverna* and invites Jack and me to join him. "It's an amazing spectacle," he says. "Completely Dionysian."

And so it is. The sound of the *bazouki*, its pounding sexuality, so different here, under the canopy of grapevines, than in Maria's kitchen. The men, mostly sailors, mostly young, stare at us from their small square tables amid clouds of cigarette smoke. We are the only foreigners this evening, and I am the only woman. As the levels in the bottles of *ouzo* drop, the sailors begin to dance—two, three or four at a time in an elegant *hassapico*. Then the tempo changes and a single sailor walks slowly to the floor and begins to dance by himself, slowly at first, crouched and balanced on one foot, then turning, controlled and precise. The music speeds up and soon he is spinning and leaping and the others are shouting *oopa!* and the air is electric and plates are crashing on the floor with shards of china flying everywhere. I sit stunned and mesmerized; I have never seen anything like this before. Another dancer follows, and another. Sometimes they dance in pairs, circling each other, and it goes on for hours, the room crackling with sexuality. Jack looks amused and interested; Bryan's face is flushed and his eyes are wild. I imagine my own face mirroring his.

Another evening: Bryan appears at my door again, this time with three sailors. It is still light, women and children on the street. The sailors usually stick to the open areas around the piazza and around the *tavernas* on the other side of the harbour, so it seems odd to see them here. They stay only a few minutes. Jack is not at home and I have lessons to prepare for the next day, so I cannot go out this evening, I tell Bryan. The sailors grin at me. I am vaguely uncomfortable having them here, in my house, but I am also thrilled. They are so handsome, their eyes so brown and shining. Bryan is unusually witty and animated; he looks as if he has been drinking, though he has not. I suddenly recognize the behaviour: he is like any female in the company of a gorgeous young man who interests her.

The next day Maria tells me: it's not good to have sailors come to your house. People talk. She waves her hands around to discredit such "talkers," but I recognize that she is right. I want no limits on my freedom, but I don't wish to offend. I am an outsider, but I don't wish to remain totally apart.

Though Bryan never again brought sailors to my house, we often went to the *tavernas* together. Sometimes Basil and Marian and Jack came along. Occasionally Nora and some of the others joined us. But Bryan and I were the only ones who danced. We learned the *hassapico* sandwiched between two tall sailors.

Where I live now, in the mountains of southwest Virginia, there are people who sometimes remind me of Crete. Not long ago, at the edge of a parking-lot where I had just left my car, a man of perhaps 60 sat under a flowering crabapple tree eating his lunch from a paper bag. Blue denim overalls and a checked flannel shirt covered his lean, straight body. The lines of his face struck me, the angular jaw, high cheekbones, fierce eyes. Put him in tall boots and baggy trousers, wrap his head in a tassled cloth, loop over his shoulders a knapsack of woven wool in patterned yellow, red, black and green, and he could belong to Crete, 25 years ago.

"You've found a lovely spot to have your lunch," I called out, half expecting a *kali mera* in response.

He smiled, lifted his face to the sun. "Yep, it sure is."

Except for his clothes and voice, everything about him, the way he held himself, his private, quiet dignity, spoke of the mountain men of Crete. They would come to Iraklion and Chania from the villages with textiles to sell, huge loads of colourful goods piled high on their backs. I'd see them as they came into town, dusty with travel, steadying themselves with walking sticks. Sometimes they took buses; sometimes they rose before dawn and walked four or five hours to leave their goods at one of the shops, have a meal and a few glasses of *ouzo* at one of the *tavernas*, then walk four or five hours home again that night.

They reminded me of big glossy cats. The way cats always pick the best spots to sun themselves. The way they watch you with a mixture of reserve and curiosity, their eyes gleeming. Their independence, their contentedness. Their sense of the picturesque, this knowing how to arrange themselves on a chair or a bench, so that when you look at them, their beauty stuns you.

The sailors were like cats, too. When they linked arms and did the *hassapico* I almost swooned at their beauty. Their controlled movements, the tautness of their arms and legs. Each muscle at attention though not appearing to be. The dark uniforms that hugged their bodies, that made their legs so long, their hips so slender. And when they sat at corner tables nuzzling each other, we smiled knowingly. Everyone had a theory. The sailors were all bisexual. Or they took each other only because women were forbidden. When they finished their two years of service they would return to their cities and villages and find wives. I didn't care. I loved them collectively. Because they danced with such abandon. Because when they threw plates on the floor and yelled *"oopa"* they really meant it.

Of course I had my favourites. Two in particular, with square jaws, smooth skin and dark slender eyes. On warm, spring evenings they took turns walking me home. On the way we sometimes paused along the old seawall to watch the moon, and I would let them kiss me. They smelled of warm olives and oregano, and rubbed their hands along my back. When I felt the hand slide over my hips and begin to lift my skirt I'd say *"Oche"* and the hand would return to my back.

Though they accepted this limitation without protest, I sometimes wondered what they thought. In the west, only the shyest of boys would not press for more, would not expect more. A Greek girl, however, would not be alone with a man, would not allow him even these fairly innocent kisses unless she were a bad girl, or a prostitute. But then a bad girl or a prostitute would not tell him to stop.

I had left behind the rules and restrictions of my Catholic days—so why did I restrain them, those beautiful young men? Why did I not bring them back to soften the hard, wooden cot I slept on, to warm the nights, as, I suspected, Bryan did? I could hear one of my old friends saying: "It's your invisible chastity belt. The nuns fastened them on us bit by bit, from the time we were little girls." Even as we felt our once strong faith slipping away, we felt the presence of those belts. Guilt. Fear. Things that dampen the spirit, dull the fire.

Yet here I was in Greece, the land of fires. And lying on my wooden cot, with only my thin sleeping-bag to soften it, I wondered at my restraint. Was I choosing this as a form of self-discipline in a life I was consciously making for myself, or was I abstaining because of fear? Was it possible to discipline oneself without quenching the life force? I wanted both Apollo and Dionysius—order and unboundedness. How did the two coexist? And how could I reconcile them within myself? The answer had to be here somewhere.

5

In the first two years after I left Greece, three letters came from Maria. The first, correct and formal, was written by some unnamed person: "I hope you are Well. I can not write to you as I would like to, but only through a translation... My sister, I will not forget the pleasant time we all had here, you are a lovely girl and you love my children and I. Maybe you will come again to Crete and dance Cretan dances in my house once more. I would like you to be near, but the sea is too big and Canada too far away...." The second, written by Yannis, was short and filled with expressions of love: "My children all the day ask me where is Simone, Mother? ... You have many kisses from my children and from my grandmother. You have many kisses also from John and he has write this letter... "

The third letter was in Greek, written by Maria herself—four pages of tiny Greek script. Because I had mastered only a speaking knowledge of Greek, it lay on my desk, unread, for three long months. Finally, I found someone in the small Canadian city where I lived able to translate it. That letter, and its translation, are now lost. I remember none of its contents specifically, but I remember the tone, and I imagine Maria, those many years ago, sitting at her kitchen table. It is late afternoon, the empty time of the day when we used to dance.

She bends over the pale blue onion-skin paper, and writes out her longings. I see her compact body in its simple cotton dress, her mouth pursed, her eyes fierce and lonely.

Once, when she called me over, it was not to dance, but to show me a small worn book. The house was empty, the sky overcast. The book contained Maria's secret life—poems she had written, mostly as a girl and as a young married woman. My sister, she said, I know you will understand. I understood, in fact, few of the words, my small Greek vocabulary too narrow to encompass such expressions of yearning. But I listened anyway, watching her wistful, sorrowing face. Many of the poems were *Matinades*, a form famous in Crete—short poems, with internal rhymes intended to be spoken and accompanied by a lute or *bazouki*. Maria half sang as she recited them. When we heard someone at the door, she stole upstairs to restore the book to its hiding place.

This was the first time I had seen this part of Maria, though something in her eyes had told me it was there. And I began to look at her differently, to wonder about her. What kind of life did she have with Giorgos? Had they chosen each other, or had the marriage been arranged? What did they talk about, alone in their marriage bed? I thought of the Australian woman I'd met in the youth hostel in Iraklion who had run away from her husband and home. Did Maria, too, sometimes long for such wings?

For a long time I refused to see the dark side, refused to believe there could be a dark side to this land of light.

In mid-February, Crete begins to shed its winter coat. The rains stop, the midday sun heats up the earth, oranges ripen, anemonies erupt into bloom all over the hillsides, wild thyme and oregano release their fragrances. Someone organizes an excursion to the countryside. There are six or seven of us— American, Canadian, Irish, English, Australian; we will bring lunches, hike over the hills all day. We take a local bus to some point on the Akrotiri peninsula, a few miles from Chania, and begin walking. The sky opens up, immense. The light dazzles. We braid yellow and blue and purple anemonies into our hair. And it's all wonderful and timeless, somehow. The wild, beautiful Cretan countryside, open, unfenced, owned by the gods, it seems. After a few hours, we stop to picnic in a shaded area under a clump of trees. Somewhere a herd of goats grazes, we hear their tinkling collar bells, the heavy drone of bees. Lazy, drowsy, we share a few bottles of *retsina*, nap, talk, smell, listen. The afternoon trickles by.

We rouse ourselves and walk some more, enjoying the fragrant air, the quiet companionship, in no hurry, but hoping to find our way to a village, from which we can take a bus back to Chania before dark. The sky is deep blue, cloudless. Every bush we touch sends up a wonderful aroma. We follow a worn path, surmising that it must lead somewhere, and when we come to a wire fence, downed where the path went through, we think nothing of it and go on. From the other side of the hill we can see a town below on a bay. Huge warships lurk on the waters. "That's Souda Bay," someone says. The Greek naval station is in Souda Bay; the sailors we meet in the *tavernas* all come from there. If we can make our way down there, we can find the bus to Chania.

The path takes us to what looks like a dilapidated water tower. A young Greek dozes on a chair perched on a small, high balcony attached to the tower. "*Kali spera!*" we call out. Could you tell us how to get to Souda Bay? The young man almost falls out of his chair in astonishment. In a moment he is on the ground beside us, holding up a rifle with a bayonet. What are we doing there, he demands to know. It is forbidden! Forbidden! We are trespassing on a NATO base, he tells us.

We have all heard about the NATO base; everyone has, though its specific whereabouts are supposed to be top secret. We shrug our shoulders and tell him we simply followed a path, that the whole thing is a silly mistake. We just want to get to Souda Bay so we can catch a bus and go home.

He is very sorry, he tells us, but he will have to arrest us.

He points us down the hill, and follows us nervously, holding his bayoneted rifle at our backs. We scramble down the hill, no longer noticing the sky, the flowers, the light. How easy to fall on that steep, rocky hill, and a fallen rifle is likely to discharge. After a mile or so, we come to some barracks. More astonished faces. One of the officers speaks English.

"Look, we aren't spies!" we tell him. "We all come from NATO countries, or friends of NATO countries."

"You may have been sent to check on our security," he says, eying us narrowly. "We cannot take any chances." He examines our packs; three have cameras. He is very sorry, but he will have to take the cameras. He is sure we will understand.

We are loaded into the back of an army truck with two armed soldiers who fondle their rifles and grin at us benignly. By now, darkness is falling, and the whole thing has begun to feel surreal. This is some grade B movie, we tell ourselves; this is not really happening. And yet we have all become intensely aware of the shifting, dangerous borders that separate friend and foe, appearance and reality.

We are taken to some kind of headquarters in Souda Bay, and again questioned in English. The cameras are returned, but the film and our passports are confiscated. It is all very embarrassing, the officer assures us, shrugging his shoulders. But they have to be sure. Finally, we are told we can return to Chania, but cautioned not to leave town until the matter is resolved.

A few days later the passports are returned, though the film is not, and the unpleasantness is apparently over. For me, however, it is just beginning.

I don't remember if I told Maria about this incident. And if I did, I don't remember how she reacted. It's likely that I didn't tell her at all. I divided my life carefully into three compartments: my life with the other expatriates (mostly in the *tavernas* at night), my life with Maria and her children, and my teaching life.

At the *Instituto Amerikaniko-Helleniki* I taught three classes: a group of twelve- and thirteen-year-old boys, a co-ed class of about a dozen high school seniors preparing to take the Cambridge proficiency exams, and a group of seven or eight local merchants.

While the other shopkeepers take their meals at home, sleep with their wives, or do whatever they all do between one and four in the afternoon when the shops are closed, these men spend an hour, three afternoons a week, practicing their English with me. They range in age from their late twenties to late forties, and their manner toward me is formal. They call me "Miss," and hold doors open for me, bowing slightly, as if I were a visiting dignitary. I acknowledge their deference with a smile, wondering what their wives would think—their husbands treating a woman this way, while *they* are expected to obey and please.

We spend about half of our time in general conversation; I gently correct their grammar and pronunciation and supply words when I can guess the intent. We converse mostly about "Amerika"; they are passionately interested in "Amerika." They have heard there is a sexual revolution going on there, and they are eager to learn how it works. "In America, is it true that a girl can go alone at night with a boy who is not her brother, and her parents do not know his parents?" I am careful with my reply, aware of my position, a single woman about whom there is already too much speculation. And in Chania, the old codes still prevail: a boy who dishonours someone's sister is likely to feel a knife in his back.

"It's very different there," I tell them. "Being alone together does not necessarily mean that something shameful will happen." They wrinkle their faces in puzzlement. They would never believe that a man sleeping alone on the third floor of a house would not sometimes wander at night to the bed of a woman, sleeping alone on the second. They would never believe that a woman who dances the *hassapico* with sailors and sometimes sits on their laps, and drinks with them, and sometimes walks home alone with one and lets him kiss her, does not allow him other things as well. But all that is part of my other life, my life in the old quarter. These men never go to the old quarter.

These men live in the better part of the city, in houses with water heaters, small refrigerators, stoves. Their wives do not carry the Sunday roast to the bakery down the street to be cooked in the public oven for a few *drachma* like Maria does. Their wives wear wool and rayon instead of cotton, their coats have fur collars. And at night, when the tavernas crackle with music and the scent of grilled *brisoles* wafts through the air—when *retsina, metaxa,* and *ouzo* flow, when feet fly in dance, plates crash on the floor amid cries of "*oopa!*"—these men are at home with their wives and children.

I know this because I regularly visit such a home. On Saturday mornings I privately tutor the younger sister of one of my thirteen-year-old boys. There are no English classes for ten-year-old girls, and to send her with the boys would not be proper. The father is not among my businesssmen, but he could be; he and they are the same. My pupil's house is relatively new. The surfaces are smooth, the corners of the rooms sharp and well-defined, unlike the rooms of the houses in the old quarter. There are plenty of windows, covered with lace curtains and hung with heavy drapes of velvet and brocade. The chairs and sofas are heavy and ornate. Solid looking. In this part of town, you never see bedding flung out over the balcony to air like you do in the old quarter.

The mother is attractive in a plump, soft sort of way. She smiles sweetly and greets me graciously in spite of the cheap cotton skirts and shabby tops I wear. She, too, calls me "Miss." I call her "*Kyria*"—Mrs. Like Maria, she speaks no English and relies on her son to translate. Unlike Maria, she shows no curiosity toward me. Each time I come, she offers me tea in a flowered china cup, then leaves the money for each lesson discreetly on the sideboard, near my coat.

One Friday, the boy says to me after class: "My mother, she say no come tomorrow. Come Sunday, for to go on picnic. Three o'clock. We go to country. You come?"

When I arrive, slightly before three, they are all waiting. The children are happy to see me and the mother looks both pleased and relieved, as if she had feared that I wouldn't show. The *Kyrios*, her husband, acknowledges me with a slight nod. This is only the second time I have seen him. On the day of my first lesson with his daughter, he nodded at me on his way out. I suspect he had stayed behind to catch a glimpse of me, to make sure I was "safe," and to give his approval. A *Yaya* appears from one of the back rooms. I have not seen her before and wonder whose widowed mother she is—his or hers. It's impossible to tell. She is dressed all in black with a black wool kerchief pulled over her head like the *Yayas* in the old quarter. She is the one link between these two worlds. She is not introduced.

A big black Mercedes waits out front. The *Yaya* sits in the front with the man and woman, near the door. I sit in the back between the two children. The girl, who is still very much a beginner in English, holds my hand and looks at me adoringly. The boy keeps smiling, as if he can't believe I am really there, his English teacher, on an outing with his family. The adults sit stiffly, silently, in the front. I wonder briefly whose idea it was to invite me. The children's? The mother's?

Kyria says something in Greek to the boy, gesticulating with her head that he should tell me. "My mother she say to tell you that the orchards will be beautiful today." I smile at her: "I'm looking forward to seeing them. I am very happy that you invited me to come." She nods as I speak. She understands more English than she lets on. She translates my words to her husband and returns her eyes to the road. He glances at me through the rear-view mirror. He seems aware of me, but not aware; I am part of the women's world with which he need not concern himself.

His wife, however, pulses with awareness. Throughout the ride I feel her controlled attention. Though she speaks mostly to her husband or looks out at the countryside, she is acutely aware of what is going on in the back seat. If we all do not have a wonderful time, she will blame herself. This is my first encounter with upper middle-class Greek life, and I am carefully taking it all in, noting how different this woman is from Maria, how different they all are from the villagers I have met, and from the people in the old quarter. Maria and I would be singing by now. Laughing out loud. Exclaiming over the beauty of the hills. She would be teaching me the Greek names of things.

The girl beside me squeezes my hand. "Is good day, yes?"

There is a tacit understanding that I speak only English, so that makes it difficult to communicate with the adults. The school is total immersion, and we teachers are discouraged from admitting to any knowledge of Greek. I suspect I have been invited along to give the children a chance to practice their English. Why else? *Kyrios* and *Kyria* do not ask me about life in "Amerika," or my life here or what I think about things. And yet I feel they are studying me, discreetly.

The country house is utterly charming—whitewashed stucco and surrounded by a low stone wall. It is grander than any of the houses I saw in my wanderings around the island, though it is still relatively simple. *Kyria* points to the small outhouse, apologizing profusely for the lack of an indoor toilet. This strikes me as very funny, given my own living conditions, but I suppress my smile. Wide windows look out over row upon row of orange trees.

Huge baskets are unloaded from the trunk of the Mercedes and there is a flutter of activity. The women will not let me help and shoo me out of the kitchen. The children hover around me like bees.

"My father say to come and see the orchard," the boy says.

Kyrios stands at the door fingering his worry beads. The children and I follow him out. The day is glorious, the air dazzling in its sweetness, and I want to jump into the air and shout with joy. But I control myself, as seems to be required, and smile demurely. Two donkeys, tied to a stake by a shed stare at us with comic faces. I have a particular fondness for donkeys, and rush over to stroke their necks and ears. *Kyrios* gestures for me to get on one of them. It's the first time he has addressed me directly. The children shriek with glee when I swing my leg up over the donkey's back. They quickly climb onto the other one.

Their father takes the reins of my donkey and leads us down the rows of the orange grove. The trees are much smaller than I ever imagined they could be, with enormous bright fruit hanging heavily from the branches. *Kyrios* pulls down an orange the size of a cannonball and slices it open with a knife he pulls from his waist. Then he presents it to me with a little bow. I am reminded again how everything in Greece seems fuller, riper, bursting with life. Even the oranges are unrestrained, glorious in their hugeness, their sweetness, their intense colour. By now I have lost all reserve and exclaim aloud at the beauty of everything. "It's all so lovely! Lovely!" I tell them. "I feel like a queen!" The children find everything I say and do amusing, and laugh and laugh.

When we get back to the house we find a beautiful meal laid out on a long rectangular table in a shaded area outside—feta cheese, black olives, bread, *dolmathes, taramasalata,* two kinds of beans, several plates of things I don't recognize, and a huge bottle of *retsina*. We are all more relaxed now, more comfortable with each other. Even the *Yaya* nods and smiles. The sun beats down, waves of fragrance waft in from the orange grove. After a few glasses of *retsina, Kyrios* raises his glass and sings a few lines of a song: "*Ego tha kopso to krassi, ya sena agapi mou chrisi....*" His wife throws him a disapproving glance and mutters something, but too late. I clap my hands, delighted. A drinking song! This is the first sign of passion I've seen in these upper middle-class Greeks.

I insist on learning the song, and sing it over and over, a bit tipsy myself by this time. My pupils and their father sing it with me. *Kyria* sings a few lines herself, though she looks uncomfortable, as if she is doing something vaguely improper.

After the meal, the children and I take a last stroll through the orchard. It's a wonderful afternoon, and I am sorry when it ends.

On the way home we are again subdued, polite. My hosts ask where I live so that they can deliver me to my house. I protest that the streets are too narrow for their car, and ask to be let out by the old harbour, saying that I will walk the rest of the way. I do not want them to see where I live. I do not want them anywhere near my life there.

So it came to seem even more that money, things, were the problem. With them came propriety, reserve. Even the passionate Greeks could be dulled, their fire banked by worldly goods.

I was impressed by the orange trees, though. It didn't occur to me that they, too, were worldly goods. Didn't even the *Kyrios* fill with passion when he sat in the shade and looked out over those splendid groves?

"Cretan oranges are the most wonderful I have ever eaten," I wrote to my mother back home in Nova Scotia. "The size of cannonballs, but juicy and sweet. Nothing at all like those small, hard pulpy things we get in Halifax." I wrote to my mother regularly from Crete, my mother who had wanted all her life to travel, but who had left Eastern Canada only once, and then only to attend my college graduation in Boston. I knew she hungered for details, so I described the food, the terrain, the youth hostels, my house, the sea, the people I met. I told her about Maria, the music, the dancing. I didn't mention the long solitary walks, the agonizing internal debates. Nor did I say much about the sailors, the *tavernas*, the wild nights out.

Four years later, when she had saved enough money, my

mother came to see for herself. Her hotel in Chania, not far from the old quarter, overlooked the sea I had lovingly described. She brought small gifts for Maria and the children. She stood outside my old house and stared at it. Afterward, she sent me four photos: two show her and Maria and the children standing in front of my old house. Another shows my mother and Yannis and two of the girls standing by the old city wall, near where the gypsy camp had been. In the fourth, my mother sits on the old sea wall, touching the edge of her glasses, as if she can't quite believe what she is seeing.

Hers are the only photos of Maria and the children I have, for I owned no camera during my travels. Whenever I look at them, I am always astonished, for the photo I remember is not at all like these. Maria looks the same, but the children, after only four years, are barely recognizable. I have tried to fix their newer selves in my memory, but moments after I look away, the images shift, dissolve: my mother disappears from the pictures and the children's faces and bodies become younger. Maria and the children rearrange themselves in front of my old house as I remember them.

6

My class of twelve- and thirteen-year olds was my favourite. A teasing, affectionate relationship existed between us. They found me endlessly amusing, and I was charmed by their small compact bodies, their dark curious eyes. Once when I came into the classroom and turned on the light switch, nothing happened. I flipped it off and on several times while the boys watched me. Nothing. Things often didn't work in Greece, so I shrugged and said, "I guess we'll just have to have class in the dark today." They all burst out laughing. One of the boys climbed up on his desk and turned the lightbulb; another flicked on the switch and the room filled with light. We all laughed together. I had enjoyed this trick as much as they had, so when I walked into the classroom the day after my visit to the orange groves and felt an expectant tension in the air, I figured something was up.

One of the boys had just finished writing something in Greek on the blackboard and was hurrying back to his seat. All sixteen of them were watching me, suppressing grins.

"Aha," I say, going along with it. "Someone left me a message. Help me translate it." Titters all over the room. "It's nothing," the boy whose sister I tutor says. "I'll erase it for you." He gets up and approaches the board. But something in his face makes me want to know what the words say.

"No, let's figure it out. It'll be good practice. Let's see, the first word is..." I squint at the Greek letters and sound out *"Ego..."* Someone from the back row calls out boldly: *"Ego tha kopso to krassi."* General laughter. I glance quickly at my friend in the front row who hangs his head sheepishly. Obviously, he has told his friends about our excursion, and they have seized on the part they found most interesting.

"Oh yes, the song I learned yesterday," I say, feeling a little chilled, the private made a bit too public. "I like Greek songs. I'd like to learn a lot of them." The boys are restless, whispering things to each other, their eyes flashing a kind of wildness. One of them calls out something in Greek that I don't understand, and they all laugh again. The laughter has a new, aggressive edge.

"What did you say?" I ask him. He is silent. "Someone tell me what he said." No-one answers, and a thick tension hangs in the air. Finally, I look at my friend in the front row. He, after all, started this whole thing. I ask him evenly, "Please tell me what he said."

He swallows hard and says, "He said that perhaps you would like to learn, um...*Krevata murmura.*"

"And what, exactly, is that?"

He looks exceedingly uncomfortable, as does the rest of the class. But I persist.

"I don't know how to say in English, but it means the things a man and woman say to each other when they are in bed."

The boys are absolutely still, studying my reaction. The air crackles with danger.

"I see," I say. "Thank you for your translation." Then I turn to the rest of the class. "Take out your homework now, and let's see how well you've done on the exercises for today." I go on with the class as usual, though I smile less and make no joking asides as I usually do. Something between us has changed.

On my way home, I try to figure it out. A single woman drinking wine and singing—did this somehow mean sexual availability in the minds of these twelve- and thirteen-year old boys? The harbour water is greenish black today; two small boats, moored in the protected area, rock gently in the lapping tongues of water. Beyond the seawall, the water is deep blue; whitecaps surge and break. It's the same water; only the seawall separates it, only the seawall tames it. How easily things can turn, I think, how easily things can careen out of control.

I remember, now, a late afternoon in mid November. This is before Chania and Maria and the sailors and the *Instituto*. The days are still warm, but the nights now have a chilly edge. My companion and I are walking along a country road somewhere on the eastern end of Crete. We have been walking for hours, hoping a car or truck will pass so we can ask for a lift and find some place to buy food and spend the night. None comes. We pass an olive grove and ask two men working there whether there is a place nearby where we can spend the night. "*Monasteri*," one of them tells us, and gestures down the road.

We have heard that some monasteries will take in travellers, so this sounds promising. Tantalizing, too, is the prospect of seeing a monastery. The youth hostels in Thessaloniki and Athens were full of stories about the ancient monastery at Mount Athos. Nothing female is allowed on the peninsula, they'd said. No cows, no female sheep or goats, no hens. And certainly no girls and women. The English boys, the American boys, grinned as they told these stories. The young women who listened, did not. But this monastery had to be different, or the man would not have directed us there. I would get to see one after all.

We continue down the road a few miles, but find nothing. We are very tired, and the sun is beginning to settle on the horizon. We come upon a raggedy, unshaven old man standing by the side of the road with a donkey, and ask him the way to the monastery. He gestures that he is going there, and that we should follow him. But he does not move. He has only one eye, the other eye socket is sunken and empty. We wait with him in silence for a while, then ask again. He nods and gestures as he did before. We sit on our packs and wait. He does not look at us, keeps his good eye on the road. After a while a rickety bus appears and stops. The bus driver throws down several burlap bags and the one-eyed man piles them on the back of his donkey. Then, without a word to us, he turns and begins climbing the hill.

My companion and I follow him. By now streaks of pink are appearing in the sky. There is no path that I can see, yet our guide seems to know where he is going. He and the donkey are sure-footed, but we have to scramble to keep our foothold, and to keep up with him. As darkness begins to fall, everything becomes utterly still and silent. In the distance collar bells tinkle, letting us know that a herd of sheep or goats grazes somewhere. Our guide, always silent, never turns to look at us, to see if we are following. We stumble along in the dim light, and a deep fear rises in me. The darkness, the strangeness of our guide, this invisible path that leads on and on—we would never be able to find our way back to the road if he should lose us.

After what seems like an interminable journey, we see the faint silhouette of a roof and bell tower against the almost black sky. The one-eyed man ties up the donkey and loads the burlap bags onto his back. We follow him into a room where there is flickering light. It comes from a fire in a low, open hearth, and an old woman stoops before a huge black cauldron hung over the fire. She springs up when she sees us and says something to the one-eyed man. He gestures and nods. We realize now that he is mute. What happened to him, I suddenly wonder, to render him both mute and one-eyed? The old woman grins at us fiercely with a huge cavernous mouth and gestures that we sit. We find a spot on a low bench by the side of the wall and look around. It's hard to get a sense of the room; there are no candles, no lamps, only the light from the fire. The old woman finds something about us very amusing and cackles eerily. The whole thing reminds me of MacBeth—the witches scene. I find it both riveting and terrifying.

After a while a bell rings, and suddenly a few thin electric lights come on. The one-eyed man gestures that we follow him, and he takes us into a hall with a long table, where we are met by a monk. He wears the black robes of the Greek Orthodox priest, but he is leaner than most of the priests I have seen and his head is bare. His beard is long and unkempt, and what look like bits of food cling to it; his hair, pulled back from his balding head, is tied at the back of his neck in a low ponytail. He speaks a little English and says that they have been at prayer; now we will be fed. He explains this to my companion; not once does he look at me or even acknowledge my presence.

My companion asks him how large the monastery is, and he tells us there are only five monks now. Once there were several hundred. But the young men are not coming any more. I step a little toward him and ask a question. He backs away, standing pointedly away from me, as if I am some strange vermin and there is safety only in keeping a distance. He does not answer my question until my companion repeats it.

He is not much interested in us, asking nothing of where we come from or what brings us here, and he deals with us briskly, as if he were performing a chore, like sweeping the floor. After a few minutes he brings us each a bowl of stew and a huge hunk of bread, and leaves us at the long table to eat it by ourselves. After we have finished eating, he appears again, and leads us by lantern out through the yard to a room off the barn. There are three cots, each with a mattress of burlap-covered hay and a coarse red blanket. He gives my companion a candle and a few matches; we hear him lock the door as he leaves.

It's a strange night. There are fleas in the straw, and eventually they find their way into my sleeping bag. I spend most of the night scratching, tossing in the pitch dark that smells of hay and leather. I listen to the utter utter silence, thinking of the locked door. Thinking of those five ageing monks and the terrible danger my femaleness holds for them.

Eventually I fall into sleep, and wake to light seeping in through cracks in the wallboards. In a corner of the room are an old loom and a donkey saddle. When we try the door, we find it unlocked. No-one is around. Not even the strange old woman or the one-eyed man to offer directions so we can find our way back to the road.

We begin to walk, though we have no idea where we are headed. We come to an olive grove where we find four of the monks harvesting olives. Two are perched in the trees shaking the branches, the skirts of their habits hitched up, revealing shabby dark trousers beneath. Dropcloths of burlap spread under the trees catch the olives as they fall, and two other monks, their wide sleeves rolled up to their elbows, gather what has fallen. My companion calls out a request for directions to the road. None of the monks pauses to look at us; one points roughly, and we head that way. A breeze rustles through the silvery-green leaves and we move on.

A free woman, a woman whose sexuality is not owned or guarded by a father, husband or brother, is a dangerous thing.

Another old photograph, this one in black-and-white. Who took it? I have no idea. It must be December or January, for I am wearing my burgundy mohair sweater. I am seated at a wooden table in a small *taverna* with two young Greek males. One of them is named Giorgos—I remember this only because he had the same name as Maria's husband. They are both nineteen. They live in the old quarter; Maria knows their families. Are they still in school? Do they work in one of the shops? I don't remember. Like Maria, they are interested in foreigners, though neither of them speaks much English. Because I am a woman not much older than they, they are particularly interested in me. Sometimes they knock on my door, invite me for walks. I walk between the two of them, careful not to lean more toward one than the other. Sometimes we stop for a glass of *ouzo* and some finger foods; sometimes it's a sweet with a glass of water.

They are "showing me around," I am "Maria's friend," but I have a sense that they are courting me, each watching carefully to see if I prefer one over the other. Giorgos is heavier set than the other; his face is square, his chest broad. One of his front teeth is chipped, which gives him an oddly benign and endearing look. The other is taller, thin and wiry, his eyes dark and intense. He holds himself straight while he walks, and I am reminded of a proud male bird, a peacock, perhaps, or a Banti rooster. I am more attracted to him than to his friend, but I am careful not to show this. To be attracted to either one would be dangerous. Even I am not so stupid, so reckless. Not here in the old quarter where I live, where I am known.

They would like to have a party. They have seen American movies where groups of young people have parties and dance together to rock and roll music. But they have no place for such a gathering. From the street they eye the second floor of my house. Is there a large room up there? Would I lend it to them for an evening? They would bring everything—the music, the refreshments, chairs. The party would end at eleven; they would clean up afterwards.

Remembering Bryan and the sailors, I ask Maria: would it be proper? She hesitates. Will there be both boys and girls? Only the friends of Giorgos and the other one? Would Jack and I stay in the house during the party? Yes, yes and yes. She shrugs, is not sure, but concedes that it probably would be all right.

The party begins at eight. I have moved my personal things into the back room, and we have opened the doors that lead from the large room onto the small balcony. The two boys have set up chairs, and laid out bowls of raisins and peanuts for snacks. A small portable record player sits in the corner, along with a dozen or so American records. A group of six arrives— four boys and two girls. A little later four more arrive, three boys and a girl. And so it goes. There are at least three boys to every girl; and every girl is accompanied by a brother, or the brother of a trusted girlfriend. The girls look uncomfortable, the boys excited. This is a new experience for them all. To these seventeen- to nineteen-year olds, anything western means sophistication, freedom. But no one is willing to step too far over the old boundaries. The girls, especially, they have the most to lose.

There is a lot of scurrying around, people rushing out to get more friends, trying to recruit more girls to come. It begins to rain. The same four or five American songs bray out from the record player.

Since there are so few girls, the competition for dance partners is intense. One of the boys I do not know asks me to dance. We have just begun moving around the floor when Giorgos' friend, the lean intense one, comes over and says something sharp and terse to him. Words fly. I don't know what's up exactly since the exchanges are all in very fast Greek. Was he not invited? Is there some old anger between them? Has he done something wrong? Am I considered off-limits to anyone besides the two friends? In any case, I don't want a fight in my house. I try to intervene, and find myself shoved against the wall, out of the way. I protest loudly, but am totally ignored.

Though this is my house, and it's possible that I am the object of the quarrel, I have become invisible. This is between the men.

Fortunately, the quarrel does not come to blows. The offending young man leaves, again in a volley of words, and the dancing continues. More people come in and out, tracking in rain. They are excited, hot, the air is filled with cigarette smoke, loud western music.

Shortly after eleven, the guests leave, and the two boys begin to fold up their chairs. We turn on the overhead light and see cigarette butts and raisins ground into the wooden floor. My heart lurches. The six-inch-wide planks, made from some kind of softish wood, never varnished or painted, date back to the house's beginnings, some five or six hundred years ago. The boys sweep up, but the dark ugly splotches remain.

The ancient, despoiled by the modern. This wreckage, in one short evening. Forgive me, I whisper to the corners of the room.

7

A few weeks after the NATO Base episode an official comes to the front door: everyone who lives here must report to the police station. Jack and I are the only real inhabitants of the house, but the American boy we'd met earlier in the youth hostel, and who had been with us during our ill-fated walk, is now staying with us temporarily. What could the police want? On the way we speculate. A Greek law requires that after three months, all foreigners must report to the police station and demonstrate that they have the means to support themselves, so that they don't become a burden on the Greek people. I had made my visit and declaration three weeks before. Jack, however, had not. With his frugal ways, he has just enough money to support a six-month stay. Afraid that the officials will find his funds insufficient and send him home, he has let the three-month report date slip by.

"They're after you, Jack," we tell him. I can speak Greek better than he; I will explain things to the police, we decide.

The questioning is cursory at first. We explain our living arrangement, tell them that Jack has just "forgotten" to report, etc. etc. But soon it becomes clear that the police are more interested in me. A file appears on the desk. It has my name on it.

They point to my declaration of a few weeks earlier. Where did I get all my money, they want to know. I earned it and brought it from home, I tell them. I'd told them that when I reported, I remind them.

They nod. When you entered Greece, when you arrived at the border from Yugoslavia, you did not have this money, they say.

I assure them that I had. That it was all in travellers cheques, just as it is now. I had shown them the cheques last time. Would they like to see them again?

I caution myself to be careful. My job at the *Instituto* pays me enough to live on, so I have cashed very few cheques since entering Greece. I did not tell them about my job when I reported, however. I have no work permit, and even though I've been told that officials turn a blind eye to such a requirement—they need foreign language teachers so desperately— I cannot take the chance.

And why didn't I tell the officials at the border how much money I had, they want to know.

Because they didn't *ask* me! I exclaim.

One of them drums a pencil on the table. And where are the two Englishmen you were with at the border?

I had forgotten the scene at the border until now. I had hitchhiked from Belgium with two English boys I'd met in Brussels, and we had accepted rides from a wide variety of people along the way, arriving at the Greek border with two Turks. The Turks were refused entry (Greece and Turkey were openly fighting in Cyprus), and we were detained for questioning. They kept us for several hours, though we had no idea why. They searched the two boys and made them declare how much money they had. They looked through my backpack, but left my purse alone. Assuming, I suppose, that I "belonged" to one of the young men, they did not ask me how much money I had. I planned to travel a long time, and had, in fact, more money than the two boys combined, my folder of traveller's cheques tucked safely in a secret compartment in my purse.

All that was over three months ago. Why would they have this information here, in Chania? And what did it all mean?

I tell the Greek police: I have no idea where those boys are. We were simply travelling together. We parted in Athens. One went to Africa, I think. I have no idea where the other one went.

Then one of the officials asks: those men in Yugoslavia, before the Turks. You rode with them a long time. Who were they?

The men in Yugoslavia had had a furtive look. They talked loudly, sang openly. They spoke a little French, and that's how we had communicated. They'd bought us lunch at a roadside restaurant, flashed a wad of money and perspired a lot. One of the English boys had whispered: "They're on drugs."

So that was it. Someone had seen us with them and called ahead to the border. That's what all the fuss had been about. And the fuss had followed me here.

Again I explain that I had and have no connection with any of the people we rode with. We were hitchhiking. People gave us rides, I tell them. That's all. I examine the faces of my interrogators. They are family men, very much like the men in my English class at the *Instituto*. They do not look at me kindly, though, or show me deference. I do not think they would hold open doors for me—a single woman, always in the company of strange men.

And what did I know about the NATO base? How often do I go to Souda Bay? The questions continue for another half-hour. I know I am innocent of any wrongdoing, except perhaps, the fault of working without a permit. So why do I feel increasingly uncomfortable?

On the way home, again in the company of two men to whom I am unrelated, I feel a strange sort of fate beginning to unfold, as slowly and inexorably as that in any Greek tragedy.

An Australian family comes to Chania. It must be early March, for the days are quite warm. They are all blond in various shades; the mother and father a dark, amber blond, the son, nineteen, a deep honey blond, the daughter sixteen, a light, almost white blond. They are offbeat, not staying at the expensive Xenia hotel that has just opened behind the old quarter, but in one of the small, shabby hotels on the waterfront. The girl is big-breasted and her skirts dangle a bare six inches or so below her crotch. With her long, tanned legs and arms, her shining, blond-white hair, her pink tank top, she is a vision. I can feel the tension in the men as she walks by, though they resist staring openly at her bare shoulders, her bare, brown thighs. I am deeply embarrassed by her. And by her mother who does not see how inappropriate her daughter's dress is. The mother, whose own breasts bob braless under her loose dress. Do they not feel the tension? See how wrong this is? How dangerous?

I know they find me unfriendly. I do not join them in the evenings, though they invite me to accompany them. When I see them with some of the other foreigners in the sweet shops or strolling along the waterfront, I say hello and hurry by as if I am on some urgent errand.

They stay about a week: I am relieved when they leave. *I am not like her*, I want to say to the Greeks. I think of the message of her bare thighs. The girl, at least, had a brother and father to protect her.

Though they were not much younger than I, I felt no connection at all to the young women in my co-ed class. They could all speak English quite well, so there was the possibility of relationship. We were studying *Sons and Lovers*, a book my predecessor had chosen. I talked to them about the social constrictions of Victorian England, the pressures toward conformity, Lawrence's war against sexual repression. While some of the males showed sparks of interest, the young women picked at their nails, looked around to see if anyone was looking at them, doodled on their papers.

I sometimes wondered if my being there, a woman only a few years older than they, who had come all the way from Canada, who had studied in the States and travelled through six European countries, would make them wonder about possibilities for themselves. But they seemed uncurious about me, about the larger world. With my simple, unfashionable clothes, my uncoiffed hair, I had nothing that appealed to them.

Instead, they stared at the glossy pictures in *Elle* and *Seventeen*, looked past me out the window. They were simply marking time, waiting to marry and assume their proper roles in Greek society. I looked at their vacuous faces and thought: how easy it is when you do what is expected. How easy it is when you don't have to choose. I looked at their blank, unquestioning faces and thought of my own life: how hard it is to be free.

8

It's a few nights after my interrogation by the police—a little before midnight. I am walking near the old harbour with one of my sailor friends, and we have just come from a *taverna* where we have been dancing. I have taken his arm, and we are strolling under the streetlamps watching the light dart and play on the black, restless water. Two other sailors wearing official-looking bands on their arms and carrying nightsticks approach us. They pull aside my sailor to speak to him privately. One of them writes something down on a pad, and then they dismiss him. When he returns I ask him what that was all about, wondering if he is in some kind of trouble. He is reluctant to tell me; I have to coax him.

They are the shore patrol, he tells me, finally. They wanted his name and identification number. They have orders to report the name of any sailor I am seen with.

But why? I ask him, shocked.

He shrugs his shoulders, looks out over the water.

The next day, on my way to the *Instituto*, I notice a man in a tan raincoat who seems to be following me. A brown fedora covers his head, and dark glasses conceal his eyes. He is almost comical, a caricature of a detective from some old black-and-white movie. And suddenly he is everywhere: in the market where I buy a few eggs, cheese, fill my empty bottles with olive oil and *ouzo*; at the end of the sea wall where I have gone for a solitary walk; on the corner across from the house where I give private lessons.

When I walk down my street, Athena and her mother watch me from the balcony, whispering.

In the youth hostels in Belgium and Germany:

"You don't want to get in trouble with the law. Not in those countries."

"As far as they're concerned, you're guilty until proven innocent, not the other way around."

"They love to pick on foreign kids. They think we're all drug dealers."

"The Embassies can't help you if you get in trouble with the law, remember that."

"In some places they don't even feed the prisoners. If you don't have money to buy food, or if someone on the outside doesn't bring it to you, you starve."

"I heard of a guy who spent two years in prison in Morocco. When he got out, he was so changed nobody recognized him."

"There were these two girls who went to Turkey. They weren't even doing anything wrong. Someone tried to sell them some hash. They didn't buy any, but all the same, they disappeared. Nobody ever saw them again."

"They're probably still rotting in some Turkish prison."

"Either that, or they were sold into white slavery. There's still a lot of that, you know."

"You get picked up, and you never know what will happen."

What had they said about Greece? I strain to remember. Cannot remember.

The fierceness of the Cretans. This was the land of the bull dancers, after all. At Knossos, I sat among the ruins reading Mary Renault, imagining Theseus and Helike and Chryse, their slender, athletic bodies swinging gracefully on the horns of the bull. When I danced with the sailors in Chania, I, too, became a bull dancer. The exhilaration. The danger. Perhaps it was this, as much as anything, that drew me. If the *tavernas* had been full of women, would I have enjoyed them as much?

The stories I heard: "Crete was the only part of Greece not occupied by the Germans. They tried to take it with paratroopers, but it didn't work. Each time the paratroopers landed, the Cretans came out and attacked them with daggers, swords, pitchforks, anything they had. Then they dug holes and buried the bodies as fast as they could. No-one knows how many were killed that way. Thousands, perhaps. And no-one knows where, exactly, they're buried. The villagers won't admit it, but most of them have at least one German buried in their fields somewhere."

"Is that really true?"

"Of course, it's true. How else do you think they avoided being occupied, like the rest of Greece? The Germans finally gave up trying."

I imagine the scene: a blond German soldier, a mere youth, perhaps, drifting in the bright blue Cretan sky under a canopy of pale silk. Perhaps he has done this before, in France, or perhaps this is his first time. He stares at the scrubby hills below, the small herd of long-haired sheep, the groves of strange-looking trees, the whitewashed houses—all so unlike what he has left behind. He lands in a silver-green olive tree, the leaves brushing against him, aromatic, exotic, gropes for the releases on his parachute. Then he sees them, coming toward him with their dark eyes. The men with cotton scarves wound around their heads, their fierce eyebrows, moustaches, their trousers like pantaloons—he has never seen men like these before. And the women, their heads covered, their long colourful skirts trailing around their ankles, shouting something. And their hands, what do they all have in their hands? Before he can pull his pistol from his belt, he feels a dagger in his chest, and he is falling, falling, the leaves crushing against him, something sharp in his side now, the scent of sage, oregano, swimming in his nostrils, pressing into his astonished face.

Could these be the same people who had brought us into their homes? Who had given us bread, eggs, olives? Who wanted only to be near us, to look at us, to be our hosts?

Giorgos has hurt his leg somehow. Did it happen while he was fishing? Did he fall? Is it broken? No, it is not broken, but it is injured. Something about the veins. He cannot work now. He cannot manage the boat and the nets with that leg, even if Yannis stopped going to school and went with him to help. He has to wait until his leg is well. How long will that take? Maria doesn't know. She stares at the floor.

What does this mean? With no work, does it mean there will be no money? I am afraid to ask Maria this. Her face is tight, worried. Giorgos is home a lot, so I go there less often. We no longer dance. Maria is preoccupied with Giorgos, and I have my own troubles.

Jack is home less and less. He has started spending the night at Nora's, though she is a good ten years older than he. Nora's face is rosy and cheerful these days. She does not have an unexplained source of income. And she has never been much interested in sailors.

One of my students stood out from all the rest. I don't remember his name, so I shall call him Dimitri. He had finished his two years of compulsory military service, and hoped to study eventually at an American university. He was 23, two years older than I, and one of the few serious students in the class. While the others slouched in their chairs and stared out the windows, he sat up straight and listened to my every word. When I handed back papers, the others would barely look at them before sliding out the door; Dimitri would carefully study my remarks and ask for clarification. I often spent the fifteen minutes between classes discussing a paper or some point of English usage with him.

Unlike the others, he was full of questions. What were American universities like? How much did they cost? Which ones would I recommend? Had I read Kierkegaard? What did I think of the Theatre of the Absurd?

He was fairer than most Greeks with light brown hair, hazel eyes, skin tones not quite olive. Though he was not much taller than I, perhaps 5'6", he was slim, and good-looking in a clean-cut, intelligent sort of way. How much more sensible it would have been to be in love with him, instead of with those wild sailors who spoke no English, read no books. Yet it was to them I was attracted; they knew things with their bodies.

We are talking about Katzanzakis. Dimitri has read a few of his books. Do I know that Katzanzakis is very controversial in Greece? That some people think he tells lies about Greece? Yes, I know this, but I believe he is a great writer. That he tells the truth about important things. Has Dimitri read *The Last Temptation of Christ?* No? I have a copy, if he wishes to borrow it. Yes, he would. I will bring it on Monday, then. Too bad he can't have it now, since this is Friday, and he has the whole weekend free, he says. Would I mind if he walked home with me, so that he could get it today? I think about my house in the old quarter. The danger in bringing a Greek man there. I will ask him to wait outside, I decide, while I get the book.

The *Instituto* is about a mile from my house, and as we walk, we talk mostly about books. Watching his serious, eager face, I wonder what will become of him, this young man who in his way is trying as hard as I am to make his own life. As we come across the piazza by the harbour, our path intersects with that of a group of schoolboys on their way home. They begin calling out something to us. I do not understand the words, but I recognize the tone. Dimitri's face turns pale; he turns and shouts something at them. Undaunted, they follow us up the narrow road into my neighbourhood, their voices sharp and aggressive. We are only a few houses away from my own when a handful of rocks fly by. One grazes my ankle. Dimitri turns toward the boys, his face red with rage. Maria, hearing the ruckus, appears at her door, broom in hand. She unleashes a volley of words at the boys and rushes toward them with her broom, smacking them as if they were spiders. They flee, and in a moment it is over, the street empty. Stupid boys, she says, her voice full of contempt. Bad boys.

What was that all about? Why did they do that? I am shocked, dazed. Maria shrugs her shoulders as if to dismiss the whole thing. They are nothing but stupid schoolboys, she says, but her breathing is hard and angry and her eyes keep darting down the street.

I slip into my house and bring out the book for Dimitri. "What were they saying?" I ask him evenly. "You must tell me what they were saying."

He hesitates a moment. "They were calling you bad names."

"What bad names?" I insist.
"They were saying you are a prostitute."

And suddenly it is all falling apart, the delicate balance. The waters are churning, roiling, the darkness bubbling up everywhere. The old man with his donkey is no longer picturesque; he is simply poor. The eyes that watch me on the waterfront are no longer curious, but full of danger.

As I come around the corner, I see Maria and Athena and the woman from the bakery all talking. Their voices have an edge; clearly, they are arguing, Maria on one side, Athena and the bakery woman on the other. When they see me, they all stop talking. Maria smiles and greets me; the other two women stare at me coldly.

To Bryan and Jack:
"Perhaps I should leave. Maybe it's time for me to move on."
"Oh, I wouldn't worry. You haven't done anything."
"They think I'm a drug dealer and a prostitute, and probably a spy, too. The Mata Hari of Greece."
"Listen, we all go to the *tavernas*, and we were all on that NATO base."
"But you're not female."

Why am I leaving? Maria cannot understand this abrupt departure. I am going to Egypt, I tell her. I have always wanted to go to Egypt, and this is a good time, before the weather gets too hot. I do not tell her about the man in the trenchcoat and sunglasses who seems to be everywhere. I do not tell her how I am afraid to go to the *tavernas* now, how I feel on my ankle the heat of that stone. And the whispers. How they roar in my ears. How I have stopped sleeping.

Maria wants to give me something. She will go to the market this afternoon, after the sleep, when the shops reopen.

I must come afterwards, to receive it, so I will remember her. I tell her I don't need a gift, that I will remember her always, always. I am thinking of Giorgos' leg and the lack of money. But Maria will not hear my protests. She returns with a brooch, a small Cretan sword in a hilt, something sold to tourists as emblematic of the fierceness of Cretans, their ancient tradition of bravery and honour. I think of the German paratroopers, and reflect for a moment on those passionate twins, love and hate. I pin the brooch on my blouse and promise to wear it.

I don't remember, now, exactly how I spent my last evening. A letter to my mother mentions a farewell party with the foreigners and a last visit to a favourite *taverna*. "A sailor I know gave me a few 45s of Greek music; another gave me his picture and his worry beads." The letter describes a triumphal departure, fans cheering—the kind of thing my mother loved to hear. I remember nothing of this. Instead, I remember sitting alone on the floor behind Bill's red plastic bar, carefully packing my skirts, my blouses, the few things I had accumulated with such restraint—too much now, to fit in my backback—stuffing whatever I could in the spaces in my guitar case around the guitar. I had missed something, misunderstood something. Now even the walls of my house were full of narrow eyes.

9

In these 25 years I have turned less and less to those months, those events. To that abrupt departure that felt so like a failure. Instead, I have thought mostly of Maria.

In these 25 years, I have imagined myself as inhabiting Maria's life in much the same way that she has inhabited mine.

In a quiet moment she pauses, wonders what has become of me. When she thinks of me, it is like entering a warm, bright place.

But what remains of that younger, braver, more idealistic self? What has swum up through the layers, whole and unchanged? The years have thickened, the connections to that old self blurred. Only Maria remains luminous. Only Maria bears witness.

It is not yet dawn when our ferry pulls into port. A half-dozen other huge ferries lurk in the area. One, now loaded, begins its slow departure, its dark passengers staring silently out from the white decks. Three or four buses wait in the dark, their interiors illuminated expectantly. In the space of about fifteen minutes our entire ship is evacuated; cars and foot passengers stream out purposefully, scattering in all directions. The buses gather up groups of passengers, rev up their motors, and with a gush of black stinky smoke, they disappear. Quite suddenly the whole area is quiet.

I have no idea where we are. Twenty-five years ago, the ferry from Piraeus went only to Iralkion; to get to Chania from there, you had to take a bus. The ferries now go directly to Chania, and though we have supposedly arrived, nothing looks familiar. This is not the old Venetian harbour—I am relieved at that, for they would have had to tear down the old ramparts to make room for these huge ships. But where could we be? A few *tavernas* line the area, and only one is lit, so we head for that, carrying our small suitcase.

Other passengers have also gathered at the *taverna*. Most of them are Greek, though a handful of young, English-speaking Europeans mill around as well. Like most Greek *tavernas*, this one is half inside and half outside. We sit outside, away from the cigarette smoke. The air feels cool and I pull my jacket tightly shut. The proprietor and one helper scurry around with small trays of Greek coffee and what looks like brewed coffee. The menu on the wall mentions "American Toast," and "Nescafé," the only things I recognize, so we order that.

None of the Greeks speak English, at least no-one we have asked so far. I fumble with my phrasebook. Where are we? How do we get to Chania? Yes, this is Chania, the faces say, nodding. But where is the old harbour? This is the harbour, they shrug.

Twenty-five years ago, how did I do it? Stumbling from one country to the next with only French and English, not even a phrase book then. After a few weeks in Greece, the Greek words began to come. I think about the places in my brain where those old words still lodge, etched somewhere. Only a few phrases now find their way to my lips.

The young people from Europe also shrug: we just got here. We have no idea. But they don't seem to mind; they chat and flirt with a few young Greeks.

The coffee is powdered instant, the "American Toast," a grilled ham-and-cheese sandwich. My husband and I look at each other and laugh. But it all tastes delicious and warms us. The sun comes up, the houses and shops on the square become visible; we order more coffee and wait, surrendering to our state. This is the way it was, I remember now. You watched and waited; eventually you got where you wanted to go, found what you needed.

Another group of buses comes. People get off and on. I approach a young man who has settled himself on a bench with his pack and opened a book. He is German, but speaks English. "You are actually in Souda Bay," he says. "Chania proper is seven or eight miles away; you can take the bus from this corner."

Souda Bay. I would never have guessed. But then, there are no sailors with bayonettes, no warships waiting in the harbour. And I was here only once, at dusk, with my mind on other things.

By the time we get on the bus, it is 8.00 AM. We pass scrubby hills, huts, banana trees, a few tethered goats, the cluttered buildings and yards of the city outskirts.

I am trying to prepare myself for what I might find. Maria was 36 when I knew her; she would be 61 now. Has she become a *Yaya* like her mother, a toothless old woman who dresses all in black, who sits in the corners of her daughter's kitchen, her useful life over?

I consider again the handful of letters we exchanged, the fragile threads we hoped would keep us connected, threads woven through someone else's handwriting, someone else's words. And who was the "translator" who wrote Maria's first letter? Was it someone from the neighbourhood? Someone who knew me, but declined to identify herself? Was it someone who smiled at Maria's fervent expressions of love?

And Yannis, who wrote the second letter, who called himself by his English name, John, who sent me "many kisses" along with his mother's—did he, growing into his man's body, learn to smile at these things between women?

When my mother returned from Greece, she brought me a small package from Maria. I was married by then, and had a son. The package contained a knitted, light blue hooded cape, suitable for a three- to six-month-old. It was an exquisite thing, but too small for my growing baby. I kept it for years, hoping to have another child—a girl this time. I kept it long after I had given away all the other baby things, long after it was clear that there would be no more babies. A few years ago, I gave it to a close friend who was pregnant and carrying a daughter. I told her about Maria, what she had been in my life. And then I let it go.

The bus driver drops us in the centre of Chania, "*Centro*," but still I recognize nothing. Finally, in a small square, we see a sign with a map pointing the way to the old quarter. The sign is in English—something non-existent 25 years ago. We go down a narrow street, and suddenly the old harbour opens up before us.

From the moment I see it, I am suffused with an intense excitement. Everything is vivid, pounding into me, taking my breath away. The water, lapping against the edges of the piazza, the early morning sun glinting on everything. The old mosque still stands, the old limestone ramparts, the lighthouse; the same handful of fishing boats moor there. But everything looks newly painted; most of the buildings facing the harbour are prosperous-looking restaurants with dozens of tables, pastel tablecloths, posted menus with pictures of food, the names and prices in English, French and German. I want to study everything, compare, remember.

The first thing we must do, my husband suggests, is find a place to spend the night. *He* is carrying our small suitcase, he reminds me. A trio of young people, two young men and a young woman, each with a backpack, emerges from one of the narrow streets. The young woman has a guide book and is reading aloud from it in English. Canadians. "I'm Canadian, too," I tell them. "I was here 25 years ago." I want to sing it out over the harbour, this miraculous return, those 25 years that have suddenly thinned into nothing.

Signs advertising "Rooms for Rent" hang above many of the restaurants, but we follow the Canadian students to a pensione on the western part of the harbour, only a short distance from my old street. According to the girl's guidebook, "Meltimi" is inexpensive and clean. No, they are full, a woman tells us, but the pensione next door, the one called "Maria," has some vacant rooms.

Maria. She is there and there and there—everywhere a memory of her.

The woman next door speaks no English, and it takes us a little while to sort things out. She sends the trio to the third floor, and shows us a room on the second floor with a small balcony overlooking the harbour. The room is glorious, light and airy, and my heart leaps. It's a true Venetian house, with wide plank floors—these have been sanded and varnished—thick walls, tall, deep windows, twelve-foot high ceilings. The beds, dressers and tables are old and mismatched, but everything is scrupulously clean, with fresh white linens. It is simple and beautiful—the best of old Crete. The cost: $12.00 a night.

The woman is named Maria. I want to tell her about my Maria, but it is too difficult without language. Suddenly, it is very important that I find "my" Maria. But it is only 8.45 AM, the streets mostly deserted, the waterfront barely awake—too early to be knocking on doors. We will walk to my old street, we decide, look at my old house; later, we will look for Maria.

As we round the corner, we see a woman wearing a brown coat coming up the street. She is the only person in sight. I recognize her immediately. "Maria! Maria!" I rush toward her, shouting, jumping up and down. She is taken aback, stares at me as if I am a crazy person. *"Ego imme See-moan-ay,"* I tell her, pronouncing my name the way she used to say it. *"Polla chronia,"* many years. I don't know the word for "ago," so I point my thumb over my shoulder behind me, to indicate the past. I can hardly contain myself. I want to hug her, dance with her on the street, but still she looks at me blankly. Then I remember how much my appearance has changed. I cup my fingers around my eyes to indicate glasses, then hold my hands to the back of my waist to indicate long straight hair. *"See-moan-ay,"* I repeat. "From Canada, *Apo tin Kanadas, polla chronia!*" I hate it, hate it, that I have only these few Greek words. I count out 25 years with my hands.

Finally a slow smile spreads over her face, as if she has plucked a small memory from a distant place. *"Simonay, neh!"*; she nods her head, yes, yes. The racket I have been making attracts some attention; shutters open, and several women look out. One of them calls out to Maria, and she explains who I am. *"Polla chronia,"* she says, smiling and patting my arm. The woman nods her approval and disappears back into her house. I am almost sure this is the bakery woman from so many years ago, and recall in a flash an old scene. But this is no longer a street for whispers.

I introduce my husband, and we all study each other for a few moments, grinning. This is not the husband I wrote about to Maria long ago, but that is too complicated to explain, so I don't try. We must come to her house for coffee, she says, and we follow her down the street. She is much heavier now, short and round—portly, I might call her. Her dark hair has turned mostly grey, and her eyes are peaceful. I cannot imagine her dancing.

Maria no longer lives at the old house; fifteen years ago, she moved to another place, a few houses down on the same street. She brings us through a small parlour with a sofa and stuffed chairs—a room much too small for dancing—into a modern, bright kitchen with cabinets, an electric range, and a huge refrigerator. Except for some of the curios on the counters and walls, this could be the kitchen of any modern American or Canadian home. I gesture my amazement at all these conveniences, and Maria nods proudly. The old house was "no good," she says. She points us to the bathroom, complete with a western style tub and shower, toilet and a bidet in which some clothes are soaking. A bidet! I had worried about finding Maria in poverty, and she has a bathroom with a bidet!

Maria makes us some Greek coffee, offers us an almond cake, and shows us wedding photographs of Katina and Smaragdi and their husbands. I ask about Yannis and Ireni, for they are the two I remember most clearly. There seem to be no photos of them, but she shows us a picture of a boy, whom I understand to be Yannis' son. On the wall hangs an old photo of Giorgos, looking the way I remember him. I am trying hard to take this all in—the changes, this new and dramatic prosperity. Where had it come from? Giorgos, after all, was only a simple fisherman. And Maria herself: This sedate, comfortable woman is certainly not a *Yaya*, but neither is she the Maria I remember, the one with fierce, yearning eyes.

Maria asks us some questions, but we do not understand them. She is less patient with the kind of pantomiming we used to do and soon gives up. Yannis, alas, is not here to help. So I smile at her, pat my hand over my heart to indicate deep affection. Maria looks amused.

"*Ella,*" she says. "*Volta.*" She wants us to go somewhere with her. We link arms and walk around the old harbour. Things are busier now, store fronts opening, tourists and locals milling around. Several people call out greetings to Maria and she greets them back. They look at us curiously, but Maria does not explain. She holds herself staight and walks proudly. Clearly, being the friend of foreigners is still a mark of distinction. I am happy to give her this small gift.

In the boat yard on the eastern side of the harbour we find Giorgos at work sanding down the bottom of a small fishing boat. He looks up, surprised to see Maria arm in arm with two strangers. She points to me—does Giorgos remember? He scratches his head and grins. No, he does not, but he seems to be enjoying the game. I hear my name among Maria's words, and Giorgos nods his head. Yes, he remembers now. He smiles broadly and puts out his hand.

They talk together for a few moments, Maria recounting the details of our encounter on the street. They are easier with each other, I note, than before. Giorgos is softer, smiles more.

We must eat with them, Maria gestures. At one o'clock. At her house. She points to the number on my watch. We are to leave her now, go for a walk, *volta*, and come back at one. Someone will be there who can speak English.

We leave them discussing the fish we will eat, for Maria's hands measure out a length, and Giorgos' hands counter with another. I am amazed at how much can be communicated without words. Yes, this is how it was.

It is only a little after ten now, plenty of time to explore the old quarter. I take my husband's arm and we stroll back to my old neighbourhood. We pass the public oven, now a stylish bakery; the little store where the old man and donkey used to make deliveries is now also gentrified. Many of the old houses have become shops, or pensiones. But none of this bothers me. I am deeply deeply happy.

My old house is much as I remembered. The stucco still looks in need of repair, though the shutters have recently been painted a dark brown. The shutters are closed, so we can't sneak a look through the windows. A cat meows on the other side of the door. I remember, now, that my young friend Giorgos once brought me a kitten. I had always had cats as pets and thought it would be nice to have one here. Giorgos thought it very funny that anyone would want to hold and pet a cat—an animal useful only for catching mice. But he brought me one anyway, a straggly black and white kitten, tucked under his jacket. By the looks of the scratches on his hands and neck, the kitten had come unwillingly. I kept it in the house for a week, wooed it with saucers of milk and bits of food, but it cowered under the table, and everytime I tried to hold it, clawed at me fiercely. Finally, I gave up. I opened the door and the cat flew out to freedom.

"Even the cats are gentrified now," I laugh.

And I am thinking how like a dream all this is. Except that it's more like waking from a dream, a frightening, complicated dream where the landscape is distorted, threatening; and you wake to find everything peaceful and orderly, to find that it has been all along. Did I imagine it, then, the danger? The suffering?

We walk on up the street, past more old Venetian houses decked out with flower boxes, new paint. Everywhere we look remodelling is taking place. The old, still there, but transformed. We pass by scaffolding, the debris of torn-down walls, buckets and bags of cement. We turn off on a very narrow road, and find ourselves on the path leading to the old city wall. The whitewashed huts are just as I remember: small gardens nest between the buildings, flowers grow from old oil cans, chickens and roosters call from their cages on roofs, grapevines form graceful bowers over small pathways. We stand at the edge of the wall, where I once stood with Maria, and look down at the clearing where the Gypsies once camped. Now there is an asphalt tennis court, and in the scrubby field beside it, a pair of tethered goats. The back of the old wall remains unchanged, beautiful with tufts of grasses sprouting from small fissures.

It is time to go to Maria's, so we stop by our pensione to freshen up, and to pick up the chocolates.

I would have recognized her anywhere. Although she is now 29, her face is the same as when she was four. She speaks excellent English.

"Of course, I don't remember you," Ireni says. "I was so little. But I am very glad to see you." Her eyes are still large, expressive, and a wonderful, open smile has replaced her old somber expression.

I give Maria the chocolates and she accepts them without comment. They disappear into a cupboard.

Yannis' son is with us too, a seven- or eight-year-old with an olive complexion, dark eyebrows and honey coloured hair. Maria is taking care of him while Yannis is on holiday.

"My mother was on her way back from walking him to school when you met her," Ireni explains. "Too bad Yannis is away. I'm sure he would have loved to see you."

Maria has prepared us a feast: lovely fish that Giorgos caught this morning, fava beans, potatoes, pickled shallots, green beans, bread. Giorgos sits at the head of the table and smiles at us all, the prosperous, benevolent patriarch. Maria sits back, content to let Ireni and me do the talking.

I tell her how important Maria was to me in those old days. The wonderful memories I have of her. Ireni takes it all in, intensely interested, occasionally translating bits for her mother and Giorgos, who nod and smile.

"And the dancing! Your mother taught me nine different Greek dances!"

"Oh yes, my mother *loved* to dance!" Ireni leaves the table for a moment and reappears holding an old-fashioned boxy record player. "Remember this?" she says, her face shining with pleasure.

I gasp. "Of course! It's the very one!"

"My mother doesn't use it any more, but the boy, he sometimes plays with it when he stays here." Maria makes a shooing gesture to Ireni, as if she is mildly embarrassed at all this fuss over old things.

"And Varvara. Ask your mother if she remembers the day we went to the Gypsy camp."

Maria is surprised at my mentioning Varvara. She has forgotten that we knew each other, and only vaguely remembers that day. I tell Ireni the story, and she listens, fascinated.

"And the spiders, ask her if she remembers the spiders." I tell her about Maria's heroism, my cowardice. Yes, Maria remembers the spiders.

We talk some more, and it seems as if Ireni is more interested in the old stories than is her mother, who seems more concerned with making sure that her grandson eats a hearty lunch. And at times it seems as if I am inventing Maria's fierceness, her passion. She smiles benignly at us all, content simply to have us there. Clearly, Maria has not remembered me as I have remembered her. But somehow I am not bothered by this; I feel toward her reverence and gratitude.

Something, however, is happening between Ireni and me. I like her enormously; she leans toward me, her open, eager face so much like her mother's, 25 years ago. She is eight years older than I was when I came to Crete, I reflect. I am ten years older than Maria was then.

"And what about you," I ask. "What do you do?"

She and Yannis run a bar and small hotel on the harbour. They are partners, she tells us. Business is very good; there are many, many tourists, especially in the summer. "You must stay with us tonight if you have not already made arrangements," she says.

I tell her we are settled at a place called, of all things, "Maria."

Ireni's face opens in surprise. "That's right next door to my place, 'Meltimi.'"

Now it is my turn to be amazed. I tell her how we went there first. "It has to be some special kind of magic," I tell her. "Going straight there, as if we were drawn by an invisible hand. Then meeting your mother, the only person on the street this morning."

"Yes, it is magic," Ireni agrees, her large eyes shining.

She is poised, thoroughly modern in her loose shirt and jeans. Though she has a boyfriend and is thinking of getting married, she feels no pressure to do so. She has her own business, after all; she can do as she pleases. "My mother doesn't know we are living together," she says, winking at me.

How fearless she seems, I think, how self-contained. And how unlike the young women I taught at the *Instituto* 25 years ago. Her face sparkles with curiosity and life. Once, I thought money and possessions were part of the problem, yet prosperity has bought Ireni her freedom. Even her name sounds like irony.

The time passes far too quickly. The boy goes back to school, Ireni must go to the hotel, as she is on duty this afternoon. We plan to meet at Meltimi at six o'clock for a drink. Now Maria and Giorgos will rest.

My husband and I feel much too stuffed to lie down, and decide to go for another walk. I am thinking how wonderful this day is, how filled with grace. How if I read about this in a novel, I would say: it doesn't happen this way in life.

I am amazed at how much things are the same, and yet different. The spits of roasting meat are gone, as are the sweet shops. But the buildings are the same, only their faces have changed. We stroll along the side streets that lead to the harbour. Open fronted gift shops display calendars, guide-books, postcards. I remember how hard I searched for an English/Greek dictionary 25 years ago. The only one I was able to find was written for Greeks, with the translations of English words written in Greek letters. Now there are books translating Greek into at least two dozen languages.

There is something else, too, something I never expected to

see on Crete. Openly displayed among the postcards with scenic views of sparkling beaches and villages, are cards that can only be described as pornographic: a huge phallus; a woman's mouth on an erect penis; body parts in the act of copulating—gay and lesbian as well as heterosexual combinations. I recall the Australian girl in her skimpy clothes, the tension as she passed; the monks at the monastery; the rock that grazed my ankle. Who would have thought *this* was possible, only 25 years later? No one seems particularly shocked by the cards. The girl at the counter shrugs: "The tourists like them."

The afternoon stretches on. It seems to last days, as everything seems enchanted, precious, each moment a special individual gift. We stop to sit in a small park, for the day is now exquisitely warm. A couple passes, speaking in Greek. I grab my husband's arm: "He just asked her what time it was, and she told him. I understood every word!"

We pass through the old market, again the same. The same wares are displayed, the same huge vats of olives, nuts, oil. But everyone looks more prosperous now; more things are packaged; everything is clean. About a third of the merchants no longer close during the traditional resting time between one and four each afternoon. The old ways linger, though they are slowly dying. We stop to buy some oranges for tomorrow's travels. I open my mouth and to my astonishment, the correct Greek words come out: *"Tesseras portakalia, parakalo."* Pentimento. It is all still there, beneath the layers.

I find I have no desire to look for the *Instituto*, or the house where I tutored, or the place we held our Christmas feast, or even the *tavernas* where I used to dance. I have found Maria. I am content to stroll the old waterfront, feel the sun on my face. I am stupid with happiness at simply being here.

Later, back in our room for a rest, my husband and I make love. And I cannot remember when it has ever been so wonderful, as if we are choosing ourselves, choosing each other, choosing this moment in Greece, in Chania, with the white curtains cascading in from the balcony doors, the room full of light.

10

When we come down at six o'clock, Maria and Ireni are already situated at a table outside, looking out over the harbour. Ireni brings us each an *ouzo*, and we resume our earlier conversation.

And how is Jack, Maria asks through Ireni. At first I am not sure whom she means. Could she remember my housemate so clearly when she saw him so rarely? Oddly enough, even Ireni seems to know who he is.

"I don't know. We've never kept in touch." As the words come out of my mouth, I remember that we were supposed to be cousins. "He lives in England; I live in the States," I add quickly.

"He has come back seven or eight times," Ireni explains. "He comes here to paint, and every time, he visits my mother. Once he brought his wife."

All this seems so strange, like glimpsing a parallel, possible life. How is it I never imagined this possibility? For me it was all a fixed tableau: the past there, the present here, with nothing connecting the two. Yet, clearly, there have been other tableaux, the cast of characters arranging themselves without me.

Is this really the first time I have returned to Greece in all these years, Maria wants to know.

"Certainly!" I protest, "Otherwise, I would have come to see you!"

It's a beautiful evening, cooler now, a perfect mid-April day. The sun glints off the harbour water, waiters bustle in and out of the waterfront restaurants in a flurry of preparations for the evening meal. Everything is peaceful, pleasing. And I think again how mysterious is the trajectory of one's life. I could not have looked at Maria's life 25 years ago and seen that this was possible—Maria, sitting in a bar owned by her daughter, having a drink with friends. I could not have imagined Maria's future, any more than I could have imagined my own.

"My mother says you are always staring at her," Ireni says, laughing.

I realize this is true. I am searching her face, her eyes, for links to the past. "She was a good friend to me," I say. "I was a naïve young foreigner, and she taught me many things."

"Oh my mother loved foreigners. She was always bringing them home and feeding them and teaching them how to dance. There were so many foreigners! It was a lot of fun."

I am stung by this revelation. I think of Maria's fervent letters, how she used to call me "sister." Yet I was only one of many. Something shifts, dissolves, reassembles itself. Now it all makes sense, Maria's hesitant, lukewarm memory. I was not for her what she was for me; I have not inhabited her life the way she has inhabited mine.

"My mother has a good life, now," Ireni goes on, looking at her mother fondly. "She had trouble with her legs for a few years and had to go to a clinic in Athens. But now her legs are fine. She loves to cook, and she loves to be with her grandchildren."

I look again at Maria's placid face. She has found her place and is at peace with herself. She has made her life with what was around her, what was available. How can I begrudge her this? My own life has been full of such expediencies. Besides, I recall, I was the first of that long line of foreigners. I must have given her something of value to make her want to repeat the experience with others.

Around 7.30, Maria leaves to fix the evening meal for her grandson, and my husband goes off to explore the boatyard. Ireni and I continue to talk. We seem to have an endless supply of things to talk about.

"The harbour used to be full of sailors in the evening," I say. "I don't see any now."

"That's because they no longer have to wear their uniforms all the time," she says. "They're still around though."

"And the dancing. Do they still dance in the *tavernas* at night?"

"Yes, but only in a few nightclubs. And it's very expensive, and usually late at night."

"What do you mean, 'expensive?' Do they put it on like a show?"

"Not exactly. But the clubs have cover charges, and the drinks are very expensive. It's not like it used to be, but if you want to see it, I can tell you where to go."

"No, I think not," I tell her. I am not surprised, nor even much disappointed in the changes. It is the way of old things, and no longer important. What is here shines more brightly.

Ireni goes into the bar and comes out with an old photo album. "When I left home, my mother said I could have all the pictures of myself if I wanted them. This is a very old one. Do you know who this woman is?" The woman is standing in front of my old house with Maria and the children.

"That's my mother!" I laugh, recognizing the photo as one of the four my mother sent me years ago. "She came to visit four years after I left. She must have sent your mother this picture."

"I'm so glad to know," Ireni says. "I always wondered who she was." She looks at me and smiles again. "How strange everything is," she says.

In the photo, my mother's hands rest on the shoulders of Katina. Beside them, Ireni stands directly in front of Maria, though Maria is not touching her. Instead, Maria's left hand is tucked under Yanni's arm. He stands a full head taller than his mother, unsmiling, his arms crossed. Smaragthi stands at Yanni's left, so he is surrounded by females, not standing apart from them. They all look directly at the camera, except for my mother. She is smiling, but her head is turned, and she looks past them, toward something else. Ireni, too, is smiling.

As before, they are not at all as I remember. Instead, I see now, they are all in the process of becoming who they are now.

Around nine, Maria returns to say goodbye, for we are leaving very early in the morning. She has brought us a gift: a bag of walnuts, and a bottle of *tsicoudia,* the strong, vodka-like local liquor I was offered so often 25 years ago. We embrace, and she leaves. I have a sense of completion, something coming round full circle, as if there were no other possible ending to this story.

"You have given me some of my past," Ireni says looking at me pointedly. "I am grateful for that."

"Perhaps we will write," I say to her.

"Yes," she says, "I would like that." And I know that whether or not we do, it doesn't matter.

As my husband and I stroll the piazza examining the menus for a place to eat, the sun falls over the old ramparts, exploding the sky in pinks and oranges. And what, I wonder, has become of that younger self I expected to encounter in every corner? Has she nothing to say to me after all? Does anything remain of her? I look out over the harbour waters, thinking of the day's events, the odd turnings. Then suddenly I see her, my old self, swimming up through the years. She shimmers before me, radiant in her intense need to connect with the world, her openness to friendship and joy. This is what remains, I see now. This is what matters.

I take my husband's arm and we walk along the old sea wall. This has been the most perfect day of my life. There is nothing more I want. There is nothing I fear. For this moment, in this shining place, I am free.

Afterword: Writing "The Greece Piece"

It began, I suppose, in 1982. I was auditing a writing course taught by Ursule Molinaro; she had no car, so after class I drove her home. I was only just beginning to write seriously then, and Ursule was a real writer; alone with her on those rides, I hoped some of her talent would rub off, or I'd learn some secret about how words work.

One afternoon I told her about my backpacking in Europe and the Middle East years before, my stay on the island of Crete. I described a brave young woman traipsing through exotic lands, only half aware of the disturbances her long blond hair created. I spoke of my younger self as I would a colourful ancestor—so removed from my present self did she seem. "That was my life's big adventure," I told Ursule, realizing at that moment that it was.

"You should write about it," Ursule said simply.

I had never thought of this. It had all happened so long ago, back in 1965-66, and my experiences were episodic, they had no centre around which to build a plot. Moreover, I sensed that the real story lay beneath the surface adventures; the real story had to do with friendship, loneliness, the making of a self. I was not quite ready to deal with all that.

Years later, in 1988, after I had finished several writing projects and was looking for another, I remembered Ursule's words and decided to try writing a novel about the four months I had spent in Greece. I would make up a heroine, myself in disguise, and embellish my experiences to make them neater, more story-like. I still occasionally dreamed about my house in Chania, the crumbling cement walls, the dark rooms that became, in those dreams, a labyrinth. Something important had happened there. Something left unfinished.

I was having a hard time getting started, so I began getting up at 5.30 AM and freewriting for an hour. Someone had given me Dorothea Brande's little book, *Becoming a Writer*, and she had suggested this exercise. It wasn't easy. Awakening memory, trying to shape and select its messages, dealing with my own feelings about my younger self—and doing this all at once. I would sit there watching the sky lighten against the window over my desk, my stomach tight, my brow throbbing, an urge to run out of the room rippling through my arms and legs.

Over a period of several weeks, I wrote twenty pages. In the opening scene, a North American woman negotiates with a Greek merchant over the price of a silver and turquoise bracelet. After a good deal of haggling, they settle on a price. Then suddenly they become good friends, in the way this happens in Greece. On the way home, with her new bracelet on her arm, Joanna berates herself: you didn't *need* it. In this way I introduce the theme of material things and Joanna's (my) ambivalence toward them. The day is overcast, damp and chilly, corresponding to Joanna's mood, but also to many days I actually remember in Crete.

Joanna goes home to her Venetian house in the old quarter and is met by her housemate, a bearded British artist (Jack), who is drying his socks by the charcoal brazier, the only source of heat. Relentlessly cheerful, Jack provides a sharp contrast to Joanna's gloominess. Joanna wishes she were in love with him. How much nicer life would be if she loved someone and someone loved her. It rains all night.

The next morning, after a chill, dreary night huddled in her sleeping-bag, Joanna wakes to the sound of her neighbour, Maria, calling her name. When she throws open the shutters, sunlight and warm air rush in. Joanna looks at the brilliant sky, at Maria's short square body, at the long narrow street bustling with activity, and is overtaken with joy.

This is as far as I got. How to develop all the threads? How to tell what happened and make it dramatic without doing injustice to the static-like quality of much of my life there?

I put the twenty pages away and forgot about them.

In 1991 my husband had a sabbatical and between his research trips, we decided to make a quick trip to Greece and Turkey. My husband had spent two years in Turkey in the late sixties helping to set up a land-grant style university, so we each had important memories associated with the two countries.

From the moment we decided on the trip, images of Maria and Chania began trickling steadily up from the past. One afternoon I hunted through an old trunk and found Maria's thin blue airmail letters with the spidery black handwriting. As I read them, I heard Maria's voice, saw her large sad eyes, and was seized with a deep need to see her again. I couldn't remember her last name, and because it was written in Greek script that I could not decipher, I tore off the small piece of envelope with her name and address in case I would have to inquire about her. I remembered that our street was named after El Greco—his Greek name—and though I could still see every detail of the houses and shops, the name eluded me. Fortunately, it was there on the envelope, under Maria's name.

What happened during our visit to Crete is described in the memoir.

After Crete, my husband and I went on to Turkey. In Istanbul, the sister of an old friend, a woman we barely knew, gave us a present—an old brass coffee grinder, almost exactly like the one Varvara had used 25 years before. Such an odd coincidence, I remember thinking. So many wonderful coincidences on this trip. We were busy with visiting and buying gifts, so I forgot about the grinder.

When we returned home, I was once again struck by the need to write about my time in Greece. But how? Months passed. At Christmas, I sent cards and letters to both Maria and Ireni, telling them how much our reunion had meant to me. In mid-January, a Christmas card and letter arrived from Ireni. "You must know," she said, "that always, since I've met you, I've been thinking about you." Her words reminded me piercingly of Maria's letters years ago. As I sat at the kitchen table reading and rereading Ireni's letter, my body felt as if it were literally bursting with memory, with the need *to tell*. The faces of Maria and the children as they had been long ago swam before me. I went up to my study and began writing: "In the photo, Maria looks straight at the camera..."

I wrote as far as the dancing scene. Exhilarated and a bit dazed, I went downstairs to make some tea. As I waited for the water to boil, I thought of the day Maria took me to the gypsy camp. I pulled out the coffee grinder the woman in Istanbul had given us and examined it. There was still a little coffee in it, powdered to make Turkish coffee, which is what Greek and gypsy coffee actually is. Suddenly the coffee grinder became like Proust's madeleine: I found myself walking the narrow path down to the gypsy camp; the thin high yelp of camp dogs rang in my ears, the faces of men with high cheekbones and fierce eyes surrounded me, the smell of roasting coffee beans filled the room. I was drowning in memory. The dark lustre of Varvara's hair, the feel of the thick rugs on the floor of the tent—details I had not thought about in decades roiled around me. I rushed upstairs and wrote about Varvara and the coffee.

I was thrilled with what I had written and went over it several times in the next few weeks, polishing the prose. But where to go from there? What was this thing, anyway? It had come from the need to tell; it wasn't trying to *be* anything.

I remembered my old attempt at writing a novel set in Greece, found my old computer file and printed it out. But it was not where I wanted to go anymore. I was fascinated, now, with memory.

I had kept no journal during that year of travel—something I berated myself for now. I hadn't even taken pictures. This had been deliberate. I wanted everything to be *in* me, not *outside*. I wanted memory to be part of my flesh.

I did, however, write letters. Lots of them. To my mother, my sister, and to a whole collection of girlfriends and boyfriends in Canada and the United States. I wrote, now, to my mother and sister and to the few friends from that era I am still close to: "Send my old letters," I begged, "if you still have them."

In the meantime, I wrote another section or two of text, and then stopped. I was stuck, just as I had been with the novel.

After a few months of despair and silence, I began writing down fragments. Whatever I remembered from that time, however small. I had to get it out. I could shape it into something later, I told myself. Often, I found, what started as a tiny memory bloomed into an entire scene. From the memory of stains on the ancient wood floor came the night of the party, the faces of the girls in the protection of their brothers, the near-fight, the persistent rain. It was like yanking at a small string and having a huge fish come up.

Finally, six letters came from my mother. I remember staring at them, the pale-blue airmail envelopes, the tissue paper, the Greek stamps, my handwriting. I was awed by them, and a little afraid. They were like apparitions—my own voice, my own thoughts from the past, a direct line to the person I had been 25 years before. What I remembered of that younger self sometimes embarrassed me, her naïveté, her awkwardness. But her idealism drew me, even as it reproached me. The girl who wanted nothing and the middle-aged woman secure in her comforts—how could they be the same person? With the letters, I would have to confront that old self, uncover her truth, measure the width of my betrayal.

I put the letters in chronological order and read the first one. I was struck by the tone of voice. It was cheerful, happy-go-lucky. A girl on a lark, having a blast, eager to share her adventures. There was none of the sadness, the loneliness, the groping searches I remembered. How could this be? As I read on, I concluded that the person writing was really a persona—one I had consciously developed for my mother and my friends. I was giving them surface. But what a surface it was—full of details and impressions, sights and sounds.

When I read that first letter, I had just finished writing about my arrival in Chania. I hadn't remembered that the youth hostel was a boys' school and that only a shower curtain separated our sleeping quarters from the classroom. I'd remembered being stared at by bunches of schoolboys, but couldn't quite place the circumstances. Reading my younger self telling it made it all come back—and more. I remembered, then, the middle-aged schoolmaster with his patient, wide brow and questioning eyes. But the elderly woman described in the letter, a friend of the schoolmaster, who had written six books of philosophy—who was she? No face emerged.

I went back to my manuscript and added the shower curtain, the staring boys. I did not mention the woman.

I read the letters one at a time, carefully, reverently. Sometimes weeks passed between reading one letter and another. They were rich, heady stuff, and I took them into my present slowly, cautiously. Besides memory, there was that carefree persona to deal with. How reconcile them to each other? How reconcile them to my present, middle-aged self? So many fragments that had to be integrated. Who and what was the real self?

Generally, I tried to write whatever I remembered of a particular period *before* reading the letter I wrote during that period. It was like tuning a guitar string before sounding the pitch pipe. While I was amazed at how much I actually remembered, I was also struck by what I could not recall even with the help of my own words, leaping up from the page. The most important thing that I do not remember has to do with my leave-taking. To my mother I wrote, "We had quite a send-off when we left.... we had one last dinner with all the 'arty' colony of English-speaking people, and one last wild night at a 'joint' we all go to..." I remember nothing of this. I remember only the fear, the sadness. So which is real? Those parties must have occurred, and I am sure I made the most of them, singing and dancing. The persona again.

I have no doubt that if a needle were to be inserted into a part of my brain all those forgotten things would pop to the surface. But they are too far buried, now, ever to call back.

So what does this mean? That those forgotten things are not important? Without the direct link of memory, I cannot know. I chose to leave them out.

In June, 1992, I spent two weeks at the Virginia Centre for the Creative Arts, an artist's colony, where I was determined to finish "My Greece Piece," as I had come to call it. I wrote and wrote, overwhelmed by memory. Even when I lay down to rest on the cot in my studio, waves of images floated over me. Bryan—whose name I hadn't thought of in decades—appearing giddily at my door arm-in-arm with the dark-eyed young sailors. The smell of roasting meat drifting out over the harbour. The way the sea urchins looked in their spiky shells. I was swimming in a deep, rich river, grabbing hold of whatever I could. Sometimes I forgot where I was.

About half of the manuscript was written at VCCA. In those two weeks I wrote as much as I had written in the previous five months. But it was still all fragments. Pieces that had to be fit together into some coherent whole. During my last few days at VCCA I contemplated this. One entire wall of my studio was made out of bulletin board-type white tiles, and a previous occupant had left an assortment of colourful thumbtacks. This gave me an idea. I printed out the whole manuscript and pinned all the pieces up on the wall. Then I began arranging and rearranging. I'd read through the whole thing, then push this piece over here, that piece over there. It seemed as if the pieces could go anywhere—or nowhere. I didn't want a straight chronology; I wanted memory to overtake the present, like it had for me. But the manuscript still needed some kind of order, and that order seemed to escape me. A visual artist friend came by one day to take pictures. On an impulse, I got up and stood against my wall of manuscript, arms outstretched.

I was making a manuscript, but I was also making a self.

My "Greece Piece" still had no real title. Sometimes I called it "Maria" but that didn't seem to be the true focus. One evening I read from the manuscript, including the part about Katzanzakis's grave. A young poet came up to me after and we talked about its lack of a title. "Why don't you use the Katzanzakis quote?" he said. "'I want nothing, I fear nothing, I am free.' That seems to be what the whole thing is about." I went back to my studio and thought about this. He was right. My younger self was looking for freedom, trying to make herself want nothing and fear nothing, in order to find it. The fact that Katzanzakis had found his freedom in death added an additional irony, one that had escaped the notice of my younger self. The title stuck for a while, though I later changed it again.

When my residency at VCCA ended, I found re-entry into normal life extremely difficult. I was still living in Chania in 1966, and memory was more real than anything around me. For days I was unable even to make up a decent grocery list. I'd be on my way to the store and find that I had passed it. I'd have been thinking about the market in Chania, how the olives looked, shining out from huge glass jars. Gradually, painfully, the present asserted itself again.

I spent the rest of the summer shuffling parts, trying to find that elusive order. One afternoon I went looking for the old photos my mother had taken when she visited Maria in Crete. They were not at all as I had remembered them. Yannis was tall, the children were laughing. Their skirts were *short*. How could that be? After I thought about this for a while I realized that my mother's visit was four whole years after I had left. 1970. By then the hemlines had shot up, even in Crete. But why did I remember sombre expressions where the photos clearly showed them all smiling happily? Had I imagined the sadness in their lives? I pulled out Maria's letters again and reread them. No, I had not imagined it. My mother's experience of the family, the one caught by the camera, was not *my* experience of them. And memory had conveniently replaced the celluloid image with its own. I went back to the beginning of my text and changed it: "In a photo *I remember*..."

By the end of January the piece was finished, almost exactly a year after I had begun it. In March, I received a package and letter from my sister in Halifax. "I was cleaning out my basement and found these. Do you still want them?" More letters, with postmarks from Greece, Egypt, Lebanon. I was afraid to look at them. What if they were full of things I had not talked about in my memoir? Would I have to open the thing up all over again and integrate yet another layer of truth? I approached them cautiously. To my surprise, the tone of those letters was different from the tone in the letters to my mother. It was more natural, more authentic.

My sister had married at eighteen and was the mother of three by the time I embarked on my adventures. She had married a Lebanese man eleven years older than herself. There was a poignancy about her life that struck me. While I was off galivanting, she kept house, kept children, kept a husband. She was only a year and a half older than I, and her hands were cracked from too many dishes, too many washloads of diapers. I was travelling for her, too, as well as for my mother.

From Greece, I went on, eventually, to Lebanon, to the small village in the mountains where my sister's husband's sisters and their families lived, as well as the whole extended family of cousins and uncles. My sister had never met them. I went there because she couldn't, and described everything in great detail. That was my job.

The letters to my sister from Greece contained no new revelations, but they made me consider the whole matter of personas again. The persona who wrote to my mother was a small part of myself—pushed forward because that's what my mother wanted, that's what would reassure her, please her. The persona who wrote to my sister represented a larger part of myself—more level-headed, less breathy—but still only a part. The real self, I have come to believe, is memory. And that is what I put in my memoir.